to nancy
Enjoy!

The Golden Madonna

A Novel by

Malcolm Mahr

 **TREASURE COAST** PRESS

Fort Pierce, FL 34949
TCP27@aol.com

ISBN: 978-0-9660235-6-5
Printed in the United States of America

For Fran

Also by Malcolm Mahr

FICTION

The Hostage
The Einstein Project
The Orange Blossom Mob
The Return of the Scorpion
The Secret Diary of Marco Polo
Murder at the Paradise Spa
The Da Vinci Deception

NONFICTION

How to Win in the Yellow Pages
What Makes a Marriage Work
You're Retired Now. Relax.

The Golden Madonna

There is no way of getting away from treasure
once it fastens itself upon your mind.
—Joseph Conrad, *Nostromo*, 1904

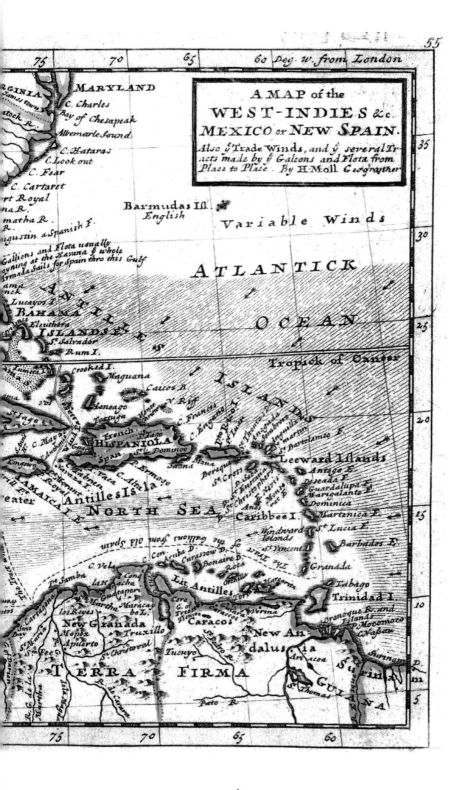

ORDER FROM THE KING
PROJECTO OF THE CROWN
TO THE COUNCIL OF INDIES
3 MARCH 1712

WITH REGARD TO THE RETURN OF THE SAID FLEET, IT SHALL REMAIN FOR HIS MAJESTY TO SEND CONFIDENTIAL ORDERS WHEN NEEDED AND ALSO TO ADVISE THE RICHES WHICH THEY ARE TO BRING FOR THE DUCHESS OF PARMA AND THE ROYAL EXCHEQUER, AND HOW MUCH SHOULD BE CARRIED IN EACH NAMED VESSEL.

IN ADDITION, SPECIAL CARE SHALL BE EXERCISED IN THE TRANSPORT OF THE GOLD LIFE-SIZED STATUE OF "OUR LADY." THE COUNCIL SHALL ISSUE WHATEVER ORDERS MIGHT SEEM APPROPRIATE WITH REGARD TO THEIR FEES AND OTHER FISCAL MATTERS.

...Introduction

To those of you who seek lost objects of history,
I wish you the best of luck.
They are out there, and they are whispering.

— Clive Cussler, *The Sea Hunters*

THE 16TH AND 17TH CENTURIES were an Age of Exploration, an age in which European adventurers embarked on "the vast green sea of darkness" to discover the *Mundus Novus* — the New World.

Despite the fact that history glamorized this age of European exploration, it was an age of exploitation and greed. Spanish conquistadors under the command of Francisco Pizarro destroyed the Incan Empire in Peru. Cortez conquered the Aztecs in Mexico.

In two and one-half centuries, Spain looted the New World of over $40 billion worth of gold and silver, which was transported back to Spain along an ocean route called the Golden Highway.

On July 31, 1715, a savage hurricane swept across the Florida Straits, catching in its path a twelve-vessel Spanish treasure fleet bound for Spain carrying over 14 million pesos in declared treasure and undeclared contraband, all together approximately $418 million at today's value. One ship, the French vessel *Grifon*, survived. The rest of the fleet disintegrated on the jagged coral reefs between Fort Pierce and Sebastian Inlet. Over 700 people lost their lives in the storm.

After 300 years, these Spanish shipwrecks continue to yield valuable finds, especially following hurricanes like Frances and Jeanne, which scoured the sea bottom off Hutchinson Island.

This story is about the lust for gold and treasure, its conquest, and the loss in ships wrecked off the Treasure Coast, of life as it was and as it is for treasure hunters who continue to seek their fortunes under the sea in quest of the 1715 fleet galleons.

Satellite Photo of Hurricane Frances (NASA)

Hurricane Frances, a super-sized storm, hit Florida on September 5th, 2004. Frances' vast breadth was exceptional. The storm's maximum wind speeds peaked at 145 miles per hour, achieving Category 4 on the hurricane scale. The center of the eye of Frances made landfall along the Florida coast near Sewall's Point, Jensen Beach, and Fort Pierce.

Three weeks later, Jeanne, another hurricane, made landfall near where Frances had come ashore, causing beach erosion and strong currents that shifted sand and scoured the sea bottom.

Satellite Photo of Hurricane Jeanne (NASA)

A reef line runs parallel to shore east of Hutchinson Island, a sanded-over rocky ridge just off Frederick Douglass Beach.

Thirty feet below the surface, embedded under the sand, a six-inch thick timber strained to break loose. Ever so slowly it tore away at the fibers until, with a jerk, the wood broke and it was free. The broken piece of waterlogged timber tumbled end over end, dislodging an 8-foot religious artifact from the silent grave where she had rested for three centuries.

PART I

THE BLOOD RED SKY

...1

THE SKY WAS STAINED BLOOD RED and so was the water as the helpless diver bled from his mouth, ears and nose. The man clutched at his throat. He could not breathe. First a sharp knife had severed his hookah air hose, and then something tugged taut around his neck. Unyielding. He struggled. His strong body arched in the water. He brought his arms up, trying to dig his fingers under the garrote, but it was no use.

The sudden and violent compression of his windpipe caused buzzing in his ears and vertigo. He clenched his fists, thrashing wildly back and forth as the loop tightened and tightened and tightened.

The face of the dark form behind him smiled a morbid smile.

The diver struggled helplessly. No matter how powerful his body, it was not possible to free himself from the lethal noose. Blood and water filled his lungs; his vision faded. His eyes went flat. The tingling feeling in his body revolved into numbness. His spine relaxed. There was no more pain, and the darkness enveloped him.

A barracuda hung like a silent sentinel twenty feet away.

Against the darkened horizon, daylight emerged.

The time was 06:44, July 30th.

THE DEAD MAN'S EYES WERE OPEN. County Medical Examiner Dr. Miriam Jolson scrutinized the body carefully, making notes in a black leather book: *3 p.m. July 30th, Riverwalk Boat Ramp*. She heard police sirens on A1A.

It had started to rain at noon, at first heavily, then in a steady drizzle which was now tapering off. But the sky was still overcast and dark. Despite the rain, a cluster of curious bystanders hovered nearby.

The drowned man looked to be solidly built, well over six feet tall, with the broad, muscular shoulders of a swimmer. His body was slumped on the ground, grotesquely contorted, mouth agape. His skin was gray wax, his face a ghostly white except for purplish bruise marks on his throat. The cornea of each eye was roughed with hemorrhage.

Louis Brumberg, the Fort Pierce police chief, peered over the medical examiner's shoulder like an umpire hovering over a baseball catcher.

"Fisherman found the body about an hour ago off Bathtub Beach," Brumberg said. "He seems pretty well intact—couldn't have been in the water long."

Jolson ignored him, engrossed in her work. "I don't want to corrupt the autopsy by poking around too much," Jolson said. "Notice the dark purple ligature marks above his Adam's apple. This kind of hemorrhaging is associated with ligature strangulation."

She unpacked an L-shaped ruler and camera.

Brumberg pretended not to notice her sulkiness.

"It looks like the man's windpipe was crushed with a garrote. The dark discoloration on the right side of his neck indicates the garrote was knotted. I want to measure and photograph the bruise markings. After the prints are developed and enlarged, I'll send them to pathology."

Miriam Jolson donned plastic gloves, knelt down and flashed her penlight in the victim's face. "His nose was recently broken. His tongue and larynx are enlarged, also indicating strangulation."

Jolson wrote an entry in her notebook and pushed the hair off her forehead. In her late forties, Dr. Miriam Jolson was attractive and unmarried. She had served in Afghanistan with the Florida National Guard and two years in Peru with *Médecins Sans Frontières*, Doctors Without Borders.

Small beads of perspiration glistened on her upper lip. "Face it, Brumberg, the guy was murdered, strangled; his regulator line was severed with a sharp knife. I'll send these particles to the lab in Orlando for identification."

The police chief was a short, squat man in his sixties, with a ruddy face and thinning, dandruff-spotted gray hair. Brumberg noticed news vans assembled in the parking area, their microwave towers cranked up, getting ready for the five o'clock report.

"Is there any way this could have been an accident?"

"Drunks and inexperienced divers might get tangled in ropes or their regulator lines. This guy doesn't fit that description."

"Could the victim have been strangled and then his body dumped overboard?"

She shook her head. "Something bizarre is going on here."

BOATER'S DEATH CALLED SUSPICIOUS

—Scripps Newspapers, Ft. Pierce. July 31. Florida's two-day lobster season was marred by the drowning of a diver south of Fort Pierce Inlet yesterday. Authorities are continuing to investigate how 50-year-old Campbell Lawrence died after his body and boat were found. Fort Pierce police received a call about 1 p.m. Wednesday when a 25-foot boat with nobody on it washed ashore at Jensen Beach.

A few hours later a charter fishing boat captain discovered Mr. Lawrence's body floating offshore of Bathtub Beach on South Hutchinson Island.

"Lawrence's wallet and other personal items were found on the boat," Fort Pierce Police Captain Louis Brumberg said. "It didn't appear that there was anything suspicious about the circumstances. The seas weren't rough, and there was no damage to the boat."

Every July the coastal areas of Florida are flooded with lobster hunters trying to get their share of the year's bounty. The two-day lobster season is always the last Wednesday and Thursday in July.

Campbell Lawrence's death brings the number of lobster diving fatalities in Florida this year to eight. Lobster hunting season can be an annual treacherous mix of inexperienced divers, unfamiliar waters and underestimated exertion.

Lawrence's body was taken to the Riverwalk Boat Ramp, where paramedics were waiting. Medical Examiner Dr. Miriam Jolson ruled the death a suspicious drowning.

...4

STAMFORD, CONNECTICUT WAS THE HOME of the Lazarus Corporation, the world's largest gold producer, with significant assets in Peru, Indonesia and Ghana.

Two months earlier, on June 28th, a man with a deep tan had stepped out of a cab and entered Lazarus Corporation headquarters at 27 Gatehouse Road. He was tall, solidly built, in his early fifties, with receding sandy-colored hair. The man wore baggy khaki trousers and a blue denim shirt and carried a worn-looking brown leather briefcase.

Inquisitive ash-gray eyes flickered behind the receptionist's steel-rimmed glasses. Her cleavage was remarkable.

"Campbell Lawrence to see Mr. Posner."

"Is Mr. Posner expecting you?"

Lawrence opened his briefcase and extracted a bracelet of small, gray-colored shells. "*Parvilucina costata.* These are rare clamshells from Venezuela's Las Aves archipelago. I dug them while salvaging a treasure wreck." He grinned. "I'm at the Sheraton. How about meeting later for a drink?"

"Wampum worked 400 years ago, pilgrim," she sniffed. "Today Stamford women are into gold and diamonds. Now, do you want to ogle my tits or see Mr. Posner?"

SHELDON POSNER WAS A PORTLY, square-faced, shaggy-haired man in his early seventies. He sat behind a large desk signing papers. Without looking up, he motioned Lawrence to a seat in front of the desk. He sounded rushed and in a bad mood.

"What do you got for me?"

"Mr. Posner, I'm a professional salvage operator. I started diving when I was a kid, working with Mel Fisher on the *Atocha* shipwreck off Key West in—"

Posner broke in. "What did they net?"

"Roughly $400 million. Even after years in court, the Fisher family, investors and lawyers became millionaires."

"What did *you* take home?"

"Sunstroke and experience."

Posner studied the workhorse of a man seated across from him. His blue eyes were cold, humorless. He had learned over years of negotiation that silence was a tactical asset.

Lawrence felt pressured to fill the silence. "I got a degree in nautical archeology at Texas A&M and joined Odyssey Marine Exploration out of Tampa. Odyssey specialized in salvaging deep-ocean shipwrecks."

Posner sighed heavily. "Congratulations. Sounds like you have a good job."

"We were working a wreck off Portugal and hit the jackpot—600,000 silver coins weighing more than 17 tons. Probably the largest collection of coins ever excavated from a deep-ocean site, valued at over 500 million."

"Dollars?"

"Yes, 500 million dollars. And it all turned to shit."

Posner studied the younger man.

"After Odyssey spent a bundle salvaging the wreck, Spain filed a claim arguing that the treasure originated from a 36-gun Spanish frigate sunk off Portugal in 1804 following a battle with four British navy ships.

"According to international maritime law, the Doctrine of Sovereign Immunity, active-duty naval vessels on a noncommercial mission remain the property of the countries that commissioned them. Spain claimed the recovered treasure—and after a five-year court battle, the bastards won the case."

"What has this to do with anything?"

"I worked on a percentage of the take, so in 2013 I ended up again with nothing. Now I'm going into business for myself, and I know where gold can be salvaged."

"I'm listening."

"The coastline from the Sebastian Inlet to Fort Pierce, Florida, is littered with beer cans, broken fishing gear, and the remains of a Spanish armada of 12 ships sunk in a hurricane in 1715. Based on manifests alone, they were loaded with $400 million in gold, silver and jewels.

"Seven of the wrecks were identified. Professional salvors worked the area for years. But that was before the last two hurricanes, which caused some shifting on the sea bottom. At this point I'm not going into details of how I know what I know."

Lawrence removed a picture from his briefcase.

"I was diving off Fort Pierce and saw a sight few people have ever seen. In a deep trench between two rocks, I saw something glowing yellow under the sand. I put my head down near the object and brushed the sandy crust away. It took a few minutes for the current to carry off the sediment. I surfaced to get my camera. Take a look."

Sheldon Posner propped his elbows on the edge of his desk and studied the photograph.

Lawrence added, "This is a solid gold Madonna and Child. The Spaniards had a passion for keeping records and notarizing everything. Their archives identify a statue being commissioned by King Philip IV. The artifact was registered as 8 feet long and weighing 1800 pounds. And I know where it is."

"So why don't you go get it?"

"If I follow all the rules, I'll end up being screwed by Spain, Peru, or the State of Florida, who gets 20 percent. I intend to salvage myself, but it takes money. I need investors."

"Who doesn't? Why did you come to me?"

"I can read the *Wall Street Journal* as well as I can salvage. Your Peru operation has major problems. Your stock is off twenty percent since April. Your company has a reputation for bending the rules to earn a profit—"

"Hold it, Captain Ahab. I don't need a lecture from some out-of-work sea jockey. If you got a hand to deal, deal it."

AFTER SIX PM, THE LAZARUS CORPORATION receptionist glanced at her watch. Her boss had ordered her to hold all calls. That was hours ago. Thinking of the handsome, brash, solidly built Mr. Campbell Lawrence, she felt warmth creeping between her thighs. *The Sheraton*, she remembered.

...5

AT A SPECIAL MEETING of the Lazarus Corporation's executive committee on July 1st, Sheldon Posner looked around the boardroom. "What I'm about to tell you is off the record; no notes, no recording devices, no pillow talk."

Posner turned to a tall man with jet-black hair and ever-shifting dark eyes. "I want to introduce our new director of security, Ray Santiago. Ray was formerly with Flintlock USA, an international consulting firm."

A hard female voice broke in. "Flintlock?" The woman's hair was pulled back and braided in a no-nonsense style behind her head. Meryl Rothstein said, "Didn't a federal grand jury find Flintlock employees guilty of murder in Iraq?"

There was a momentary silence in the room

Santiago shook his head. "Flintlock was hired to protect U.S. personnel. After a car bomb exploded, our people believed embassy employees were under attack and fired in self-defense."

Meryl Rothstein eyed the man with suspicion.

Posner said, "Ray, this lady is our in-house counsel, Meryl Rothstein. Meryl tries to keep us out of prison." He spread his hands. "So far so good."

He turned to the man on his right, a large man with thick forearms and big hands folded in front of his barrel chest. "Henrik manages our Peru mining operation."

Henrik Lindbergh nodded.

"That's one of the reasons we are meeting today," Posner explained. "We have a problem in Cajamarca. The

19

Peru mine is our most productive operation. We've extracted seven billion dollars in gold. Recently, local protesters tried to block our plans to expand mining operations into a second location, which contains more than a billion dollars' worth of gold. Right, Henrik?"

Again, Lindbergh nodded.

"What's the problem?" Santiago asked.

"For the locals, Cerro Quilish is a sacred mountain. For us, Quilish is a mountain of gold—"

"Tell him about the mercury," Meryl Rothstein interrupted.

Henrik Lindbergh scowled. "Like most mining operations, we use mercury to recover microscopic bits of gold from crushed rock. It's the easiest and most cost-effective solution for gold separation. Unfortunately, one of our trucks spilled its cargo over a five-mile stretch of road around the nearby town of Choropampa. Villagers were attracted by the mercury's glimmer and picked it up and took it home. Many fell sick and ended up in hospitals with symptoms of mercury poisoning."

Meryl Rothstein said, "Mercury is highly toxic. It can cause damage to the nervous system at relatively low levels of exposure. The Peruvians can sue us in U.S. federal court for damages."

"Not going to happen," Posner said. "Any interruptions in the Cajamarca mining operation would erode our stock price."

AFTER A SHORT BREAK, Sheldon Posner tapped his coffee mug. "The next order of business concerns a contract I signed with a shipwreck salvager."

Rothstein held her hands up in a hold-it-there gesture. "I didn't see any contract."

"It was only two pages, very basic, and I don't intend to honor it anyway."

The lawyer shifted uncomfortably in her chair.

Posner smiled a thin smile. "A guy named Lawrence waltzed into my office with a story about a life-size golden statue lost when a Spanish treasure fleet sank in a hurricane off Florida's east coast hundreds of years ago. The solid gold statue, according to Lawrence, weighed about 2500 pounds; at 12 troy ounces per troy pound, that's 30 thousand troy ounces."

"How much would that be in dollars, Henrik?"

"Gold is selling today at $1179. Thirty thousand troy ounces would be worth $35,370,000."

Everyone stared at Posner.

"The guy was cagey. He said he researched this treasure for three years before he finally located it. Where? He wouldn't say."

"If he's found the gold, why does he need us?" Meryl Rothstein queried.

"Good question. He needs money to raise the golden statue—on the quiet. He wants to avoid publicity for fear Spain or Peru will get involved with lawsuits."

"If it's on the quiet, which smells fishy to me—no pun intended," Rothstein said, "what's he going to do with a large solid-gold statue?"

"We will take it to our Carolina refinery and melt it down," Posner said. "That's why he came to us."

Rothstein persisted. "How do we know it isn't a scam?"

"That's why I hired Ray."

Santiago opened a folder. "I spoke to the marina owner in Key West where Lawrence kept his boat. He said the three main things in Campbell Lawrence's life were diving, food and the ladies, and not necessarily in that order.

"Other people I interviewed said the guy was reasonably honest. He's a hard drinker and hard worker. We checked his Key West apartment for charts or notes or maps. Nothing. If he has a computer, it must be a laptop. Phone conversation transcripts are unremarkable, and Lawrence's bank account is about what you would expect from a professional diver.

"At present Lawrence is living on his boat in Fort Pierce." Santiago flipped some pages. "He is the kind of guy who could never be tied down to an eight-to-five office job. I don't see enough here to hang a lantern on him at the moment, but you never know about people."

"What were the terms of the contract?" Rothstein asked.

Posner responded, "Lawrence wanted us to upfront his expenses, and he wanted fifty percent of the market value of the gold statue, less the monies advanced."

"Why did you say that you are not honoring it?"

Posner glanced furtively at Ray Santiago.

"Some things are none of your business, Meryl, dear."

...6

FORMER FBI AGENT Frank Fernandez put his hands behind his neck and leaned back in the desk chair, staring idly up at the rotating ceiling fan. The chair was old and lumpy. The air felt muggy. On the wall behind his desk was a photograph of J. Edgar Hoover hung upside down.

Fernandez was olive complexioned, of medium height, with clothes that looked as if he had slept in them. A handsome face, tired eyes. At fifty-five, he was overweight, neglecting regular exercise, and had let his thinning brown hair grow a bit longer.

He wore sandals and faded jeans that were tight around the middle. Following a career in the Bureau, complete with physical and emotional scars, Fernandez liked the warm weather and small-town environment of Fort Pierce.

His wife and son lived across the state in Sarasota. Maris managed the Dali Museum. Contact between them had worsened over the past months because of the quiet desperation that had built between two people who had once loved each other but now had nothing in common except a son—who wasn't his. There didn't seem to be much Frank could do about it. He had given up worrying over whose fault it was.

Crime in Fort Pierce was on the rise. Budgetary considerations had forced the local mayor to trim the police force. Believing the market for security services would rise proportionately, Fernandez had purchased the assets of a small security agency. However, Fort

Pierce residents were different from their neighbors in Vero Beach to the north or Stuart to the south. The folk living west of Federal Highway in Fort Pierce didn't require professional security services. They purchased Dobermans and Smith and Wessons. Under Florida's Stand Your Ground law, anyone could invoke self-defense if he or she felt threatened. To the east, on Hutchinson Island, senior citizens frequented early bird restaurants and didn't stray from their gated communities late at night.

The office of Fernandez's Orange Blossom Security Agency was located at 505 South 2nd Street, a short walk to the Indian River Lagoon waterfront. The real estate agent had convinced Fernandez that having a security agency located at this address would give prospective clients confidence, knowing the local FBI office was on the third floor and Homeland Security leased the entire first floor. The agent had failed to mention that the rent was twice that of other available downtown locations. As a result, Fernandez was, as usual, behind in his rent. He contemplated calling his brother in Baltimore for another loan.

AT 10 A.M., FRANK'S ASSISTANT, Vesta Jones, announced in a stage whisper, "We got company." Vesta was a feisty African-American with mocha skin and peppery white hair. She was at the tail end of her forties, a retired policewoman, part pit bull and part-time choir mistress.

"Fresh coffee, Vesta?" Chief Lou Brumberg asked.

"This ain't Starbucks, and I don't work for you anymore, Lou," she grumbled. While in the police department, Vesta had kept the chief's schedule and, more often than not, told him where to be and when.

Brumberg slapped a file binder against his hip restlessly. He flopped down in an armchair and dropped the binder on Fernandez's desk.

"Let me guess," Fernandez said. "You're here to sell me tickets to the policeman's ball."

"Wish I was. How's Maris?"

Fernandez was silent for a moment. "She's pissed because I didn't move to Sarasota. I think she's seeing somebody."

"Maris was always high-spirited," Brumberg said.

An oppressive silence weighed on both men. He waited until Vesta returned. At last the chief cleared his throat and said gravely, "I have a new murder to deal with... plus a staffing problem."

Brumberg sighed. "I need a favor. My chief of detectives, Glen McCann, is putting his mother in a nursing home in Baltimore, and Denise Battle is on maternity leave." In a thick voice he added, "The mayor's put a freeze on hiring. He wants me to use—consultants."

Frank had sensed as soon as he saw the blue case file that this was what Brumberg was going to ask. But now he felt a confusing rush of emotions. He felt a thrill at the possibility of having a part of his old life again. He also understood that getting mixed up in local police politics was a no-win situation; a case not solved in the first forty-eight hours had less than a 50 percent chance of being cleared—and he would be blamed. Whether it was the CIA, FBI, Secret Service, or local police—everybody protected their turf and their ass.

"No thanks, Lou. I know a couple of private investigators in Vero Beach I can recommend, good ones that will work hard and not rip you off."

He glanced at Vesta in time to see her roll her eyes.

She sniffed. "I haven't been paid in weeks."

"Hear me out, Frank. Then decide."

Fernandez leaned back in his chair. He felt a charge of adrenaline. "Who was the victim?"

"Guy's name was Campbell Lawrence."

"Where did he live?"

"On his boat."

"And where's the victim's boat?"

"In his slip at the Fort Pierce City Marina."

"Get it raised, trailed and secured in your police lot."

Chief Brumberg grumbled, "I appreciate your help, Frank, not your attitude."

"No. That's the way Travis McGee would do it. Ever read John MacDonald?"

"Don't pay him no mind, Lou," Vesta said.

Fernandez rooted around his center desk drawer, found a blank contract, and jotted in a figure. "That's my retainer."

Brumberg shook his head. "This is Fort Pierce, pal, not Palm Beach. I can go as high as $500 and a standard hourly rate. You might need a favor from me someday, Frank, when you're out there in the cold world with no steady paycheck coming in. Are we okay on the deal?"

We're okay." He didn't add that he'd work the case for free just to be back in the life for a few days.

Brumberg stood and extended his hand. Fernandez thought he wanted to shake hands to seal the agreement.

The chief put something in his palm. Frank looked down to see a gold detective's shield. He almost smiled.

AT THE FBI, IT HAD BEEN Frank Fernandez's routine to clear his desk before starting on a new investigation. He pushed his chair back, stood up, stretched, and decided to get another cup of coffee.

When Fernandez opened the murder file folder and glanced at the black-and-white glossies of the murder victim, he fought off a wave of dizziness. He recognized the dead man, Campbell Lawrence. He stirred his coffee and drank it slowly, remembering the incident.

A month earlier, about eight p.m., he had stopped on his way home at Archie's, a beach bar on A1A. Fernandez was alone at the bar, watching a Marlins game and eating a hamburger.

A news item flashed on the screen. The U.S. Coast Guard had intercepted a boatload of Haitians trying to land on South Hutchinson Island the previous night.

He heard the guy sitting next to him say, "Fucking Voodoo lovers land here on boats carrying two chickens and another fucking relative. They're parasites looking for a free ride, and our taxes pay for it."

"Cool it, Campbell," his girlfriend had urged.

"Goddamned illegals come, not to work, but to work the system, sell drugs, fill up emergency rooms. They're no better than fucking Mexican wetbacks stealing our jobs and raping our social services for free benefits."

Frank Fernandez noted the man was large, 6 feet 2 and over 200 pounds, but he couldn't blink away the racial slurs. With a feeling of weary resignation, he turned to the guy.

"Get your facts straight, pal. Haitian and Mexican workers pay sales taxes and work for substandard wages at the shittiest jobs. Unless you're an American Indian, your people immigrated from somewhere, so cool it."

"Thanks for the update, *amigo. Vete al infierno.*"

Fernandez understood "Go to hell." He ignored it.

"I'm talking to you, *amigo*," the guy said. "Pay attention."

The waitress, a large-bosomed woman in her late fifties, refilled his coffee. "Don't pay him no mind, Frank. He's drunk."

"Hey, *amigo*. Where's your leaf blower?"

Fernandez sighed. He pushed off the bar stool with his hip and got up slowly. He visualized what had to be done: *Hit him once in the gut and again in the face, hard. Break his nose.*

The bar went silent.

Fernandez felt a heavy bear's paw resting on his shoulder. A bearded, barrel-chested giant wearing a Harley Davidson T-shirt said, "Let me handle it, Frank."

The biker sauntered over to Campbell Lawrence.

"Bar's closing, friend. Settle up your tab and vamoose."

"Who the fuck are you?"

"I'm the new sheriff in town." He pointed at three heavyset, gray-bearded men wearing bandanas and holding pool cues. "That's my deputized posse. Their badges haven't arrived yet. I ordered on Amazon."

Campbell Lawrence's face went beet red. He threw some bills on the bar and glared at Fernandez with murder in his eyes. He grabbed the girl by the arm and stomped out.

Fernandez heard the gravel in the parking lot crunch as Lawrence sped off.

"Thank you, man," he said. "But I could have handled the situation."

"Were you going to give him the old FBI break-the-index-finger-and-kick-him-in-the-balls move?"

"Something like that."

The biker shook his head. "Face it, Frank. The guy was fifty pounds heavier, ten years younger, and in better physical shape. He would have whipped your sorry ass."

Fernandez said nothing.

The biker added, "Don't miss our church service. Archie's every Sunday, 9 a.m. Truly inspiring."

FRANK FERNANDEZ STIRRED HIS COFFEE, which was now cold. It was almost noon. As he reviewed the autopsy report, he skipped weights and measurements and descriptions and went right to the summary section. The cause of death was listed as strangulation. The estimated time of death: 06:45 a.m.

County Medical Examiner, District 19
Indian River, Martin, Okeechobee, St. Lucie

DATE and HOUR AUTOPSY PERFORMED:

09/01/2015; 8:30 A.M. by Miriam Jolson, M.D.

SUMMARY REPORT OF AUTOPSY:

Name: Lawrence, Campbell
Coroner's Case #: 2470-356
Date of Birth: 03/23/65
Age: 50
Race: White
Sex: Male
Date of Death: 07-30-2015
Body identified by: D. Ingram, Fort Pierce Marina
Case # 001284-23E-2015
Investigating Agency: Ft. Pierce Police Department

EXTERNAL EXAMINATION
The body is that of a tall, well-developed white male measuring 75 inches and weighing 205 pounds, and appearing generally

consistent with the stated age of 50 years. The body is cold and unembalmed. The eyes are blue. On the decedent's neck is a deep ligature below the mandible. Ligature is nine inches wide and encircles the neck in the form of a "V" on the anterior of the neck.

INTERNAL EXAMINATION SUMMARY

Head—Central Nervous System: Autopsy shows the hyoid bone, the thyroid, and the cartilages are fractured. Severe hemorrhaging occurred from ligature in subdermal tissues of the neck. Victim drowned in his own blood.

OPINION

Time of Death: Rigor and liver mortis approximate time of death 06.45.

Immediate cause of death: Asphyxia due to ligature strangulation.

Manner of Death: Homicide

Remarks: Decedent originally presented to this office as an accidental drowning victim. Drug screen results indicate no evidence of drugs or alcohol. The presence of ligature marks on throat indicated accidental death not possible. Based on ligature size, depth and color markings, the device used to garrote victim may have been wire. FPPD detectives were notified of these findings immediately.

Conclusion of examination

St. Lucie County Medical Examiner

THE AUTOPSY REPORT CONTAINED no surprises. Fernandez moved on, leafing through the evidence analysis report. No fresh fingerprints had been found on

Lawrence's boat. He quickly turned pages in the file until he found the coroner's property list. It was a computer list of all items found on the boat or on the body. Wallet; keys; a money roll; an auto insurance card; voter's ID for Monroe County, Florida; a business card for a Sheldon Posner in Connecticut; a slip of paper with a gate entry code for Conch Harbor Marina in Key West; and a backpack containing letters, documents, and charts.

Campbell Lawrence's boat was a 30-foot, wide-beamed fish trap boat. He found no equipment listing. Also missing was any mention of a cell phone or computer.

Looking down at his yellow pad, he jotted down a short list of people to talk to.

Miriam Jolson— the Medical Examiner

D. Ingram who identified the body

The Conch Harbor Marina manager

Sheldon Posner, the man from Connecticut

Finished with the summaries, he drummed his fingers on the desk and thought about the case. It had been over a year since his last real criminal investigation. He looked down at the murder file in his hands, waiting for an idea, but nothing came through. It was too early.

The ringing of the phone broke the silence. He could see from the number it was his brother, Dr. Martin Fernandez.

"Martin? What's up?"

"Have you had your check-up?"

"Not yet."

"Frank, Johns Hopkins is in downtown Baltimore. Every Saturday night our emergency room is loaded with gunshot victims. We have data on cases like yours where retained bullet fragments are embedded too close to vital organs for safe removal. I have told you that if the fragments are not closely monitored for lead intoxication, it can lead to microcytic anemia, and that could be fatal. Since you are the only brother I'm likely to have, please go to the Cleveland Clinic in Palm Beach and have them check you over."

"I will, Martin. Thanks."

"Chelation therapy is a treatment we use at Hopkins for removing heavy metals from the blood, but it has serious risks. That is why you need to be checked regularly." Frank heard his brother exhale a tired sigh. "I will never understand why you had to join the FBI."

"It seemed the right thing to do at the time. In many ways, this is still a closed society, an Anglo-Saxon country of pale, rightwing bigots fearful that Hispanics will have lots of babies and take over their country. When I joined the Bureau, we represented sixteen percent of the population, but only seven percent of FBI personnel were Hispanic."

"I fail to see the connection. All I know is you ended up being shot twice, nearly died, and have no money in the bank—"

"Goodbye, Martin. I love you." He hung up.

VESTA JONES WALKED INTO the office—unsmiling.

"What?" Fernandez asked.

"Lawrence's boat was scuttled. Chief Brumberg thinks somebody opened the sea cocks and the boat flooded."

Fernandez felt the low pounding of a headache coming on.

...8

THE FORT PIERCE CITY MARINA OFFICE was small and cluttered, with a view through a large window of the Indian River. The office abutted a narrow gift shop stacked floor to ceiling with nautical-inspired jewelry, wall hangings of manatees, books on treasure hunting, and imitation silver cob coins and gold doubloons.

"Welcome to the marina," a young woman said. "Are you looking for a slip?" With his windswept hair, unshaven face and disheveled appearance, Frank Fernandez had been mistaken for a pleasure boater.

"Wish I was, ma'am." He flashed the gold badge. "I'm investigating the murder of Mr. Campbell Lawrence. Are you Donna Ingram?"

"Yes."

He watched her eyes widen, registering surprise and concern, a normal response to a sudden visit by the police.

Donna Ingram was just under average height, with blonde hair and dark rings under her brown eyes. Fernandez thought she was not unattractive. On her U-shaped desk was a computer, binoculars, and a framed wedding photograph, and above the desk hung a remote camera surveillance system.

Fernandez pulled a chair away from another desk and sat down. They were alone in the marina office, but he spoke softly. "Actually, I'm not officially a detective. I've been asked by Chief Brumberg to help with the case."

Fernandez could see pain and weariness in her eyes. "You identified the body?"

35

Donna fiddled with a shell bracelet. She sat straight on the edge of her chair, her knees tight together. There were small, fine drops of perspiration along her hairline.

"Campbell—Mr. Lawrence kept his boat at the marina. The police asked me to identify his body."

He sensed a high level of stress in her voice. "What can you tell me about Campbell Lawrence?"

"I don't understand."

"In a murder case, it's important to know as much about the victim as possible: his friends, enemies, routine. Whatever you can share would be appreciated."

Donna Ingram was silent a moment. She took a deep breath. "I don't think Mr. Lawrence knew many people in town. He lives—lived in Key West."

"Profession?"

"Mr. Lawrence was interested in shipwrecks. Captain Halsey White was helping him."

Fernandez jotted the name Halsey White. "Did Lawrence have visitors on his boat?"

Donna's expression was guarded, hard to read. "No. He was kind of a loner."

"When did he arrive in Fort Pierce?"

"In June."

"Did Lawrence tell you how long he planned to dock at your marina?"

"His slip was booked until the end of August. You can't salvage after that; water's choppy and there's hurricanes."

"You have binoculars and a good vantage point from your office. Were any strangers loitering around? Any ladies on board Lawrence's boat?"

No answer. The look of pain on her face was real.

"I'm just dragging a net, collecting as much information as I can, trying to get a handle on the man." Fernandez pointed to the picture frame. It was Donna as a young bride, holding a bunch of white flowers, smiling at the camera. By her side stood a blonde-haired, blue-eyed man in a full dress white Navy uniform with a chest full of medals, including the Navy SEAL trident.

"Your wedding picture?"

"That's my husband, Lieutenant Jonas Ingram."

"You married a hero. That's a lot of fruit salad he's sporting. Is your husband on active duty?"

"Jonas is assigned to Navy SEAL Team 5 out of Coronado, California." She paused, her lips tight. "With Navy SEALs, you never know where they are being sent."

"What about FaceTime and all the electronic gadgetry? I thought military personnel could stay in touch from anywhere."

"It doesn't work that way for us—anymore."

The phone rang.

Donna excused herself to take the call. "Sorry," she said to the caller. "We're filled. Slips are reserved three months in advance. Next year we're adding 137 slips to the marina. Please call back." Her hand shook as she put down the phone.

"Did Campbell Lawrence reserve his slip in advance?"

"No. Captain Halsey White asked me for a favor."

"A legend?"

"Halsey is an old time treasure hunter."

"What's his connection to Lawrence?"

She fiddled with her hands, rubbed the shell bracelet, and looked uncomfortable discussing the subject.

"Best you talk to Halsey. Do you want his number?"

"And address, please."

In these situations his suspicion outweighed his compassion. It had to.

"Mrs. Ingram," Frank Fernandez said, looking hard at her. "Mr. Lawrence's boat was scuttled. The police believe it was intentional. That's a criminal act. If you know anything at all that you've been keeping to yourself, now's the time to tell me. Do you understand?"

She nodded slowly.

He looked at his watch. He was hungry.

'I'm going next door for lunch. Care to join me?"

"I'm not hungry. Thank you." She rubbed her nose for a few seconds to mask tears gathering in the corners of her eyes.

…9

IN LATE JULY, FORT PIERCE was hot. Very hot. A welcome cool front was moving in off the coast. Frank Fernandez chose a table on the back of the deck that afforded privacy. He didn't need to look at the menu.

"Tiki Burger, medium-pink," he told the waitress. "Hold the cheese and chips, make sure the bacon is blackened, and a Guinness Black Lager."

"I'll tell the chef and hope he doesn't quit."

He took out his list, checked off Donna Ingram's name, added Halsey White's, and underlined it.

Frank punched in the number for the county medical examiner. An operator told him Dr. Jolson was at lunch. He left a message: he would see her at 3 o'clock.

Checking the Key West number, he phoned the Conch Harbor Marina. The call was picked up by an answering machine.

"My name is Frank Fernandez with the Fort Pierce Police Department. We are investigating the death of a Key West man who kept his boat at your marina." Frank paused to flip a page in his notebook. "The victim's name is Campbell Lawrence. Please call me back." He gave the number for his cell phone and hung up.

Next, Fernandez punched in the number on the business card for Sheldon Posner.

"Lazarus Corporation. How may I direct your call?"

"Sheldon Posner, please."

"Are you a client?"

"No, a policeman in Florida investigating a murder."

He heard some clicks and muffled conversation.

"Posner here. What's this all about?"

"I am Detective Fernandez with the Fort Pierce police. We are investigating the murder of a Mr. Campbell Lawrence, and—"

"Shit! Shit!" he heard the man exclaim.

"Mr. Posner. Are you there?"

"Of course I'm here. Who did it?"

"That's what I'm trying to find out. Your card was in the deceased's wallet. What was the nature of your relationship?"

Posner paused a beat. "The guy wanted me to invest in a salvaging project. The return on investment was unsatisfactory. We had no interest. Anything else? I'm a busy man."

The hamburger was cold. Frank ate two bites, finished his beer, and decided not to call Halsey White. If he had time after his visit with the medical examiner, he would pay the man a visit.

His cell phone chirped.

"Are you Fernandez, the policeman who called?"

"Right. And you are?"

"Name's Hemingway—no relation."

"I'm investigating the murder of Campbell Lawrence."

"Damned shame," Hemingway said.

"Can you tell me anything about Lawrence?"

"Camie was all right, but a bastard when he got drunk."

"Wasn't he a writer?"

"Don't know about that. As far I could tell, the main things in his life were hunting gold, food and the ladies, and not necessarily in that order."

"He liked the ladies?"

"I'll tell you what," Hemingway chuckled. "Camie Lawrence believed the way to a woman's heart, or wherever, was by giving them bracelets and necklaces made from exotic shells, which he salvaged."

Fernandez encouraged the Key West Marina manager to keep talking. "That so?"

"Yep. And then Camie would ask the lovelies to sleep with him." Hemingway laughed out loud. "From what I heard, he got his face slapped a lot, but he also got plenty of you-know-what—"

"Tell me about Lawrence's boat," Fernandez interrupted.

He heard the sound of papers being shuffled. "It was a used 2007 Grady-White Canyon 366 in good condition. Costs about $360,000 new. I don't know what Camie paid for it—probably less than half."

Fernandez remained quiet.

"The Canyon has a 420-gallon fuel capacity and a 365-statute mile range. Her draft is just 3 foot 7 inches, so even though she's big, she can navigate in shallow waters."

"Any specialized equipment?"

"I have it listed somewhere."

Fernandez glanced at his watch; it was 2:45. He was going to be late for his meeting with Dr. Miriam Jolson.

Hemingway came back on the line. "Other than the standard Grady White depth-finder and gyroscope, Camie installed a global satellite navigation system, and I helped him find a used magnetometer."

"What's that?"

"A metal detector that records magnetic anomalies. They're used by professional treasure salvagers."

"What was Lawrence doing in Fort Pierce?"

"He was looking for gold or pussy—or both."

10

THE CHIEF MEDICAL EXAMINER'S OFFICE was located in a one-story nondescript building on 35th Street at Indian River State College. Dr. Miriam Jolson's office had a narrow vertical window that looked across to another nondescript campus building. Cardboard boxes filled with files were stacked against one wall under a Haitian painting.

Fernandez took the seat opposite Dr. Jolson's drab, gray government-issue metal desk. The police chief had briefed Fernandez that Jolson was unmarried and had served a tour in Afghanistan as a captain in the Florida National Guard.

"She doesn't suffer fools gladly," Brumberg had cautioned.

"Interesting artwork," Fernandez said.

"*Revenge,* by Rigaud Benoit. Benoit was one of the supreme masters of Haitian art. He died in 1986. The Haitian government gave me this painting for helping in the 2010 earthquake."

"The woman has wings," Fernandez said.

"In Haitian folk art there are fantasies of flying witches called *loup garous*. Have you ever heard of skinshifters?"

"Afraid not."

"Myths about skinshifting creatures persist worldwide. In South America, the *chonchon* is a woman that changes into a vulture-like bird. But you didn't come here for a lecture on animal-human hybrids. What is your role in this investigation, Mr. Fernandez?"

"I'm doing a favor for Lou Brumberg." He flipped open his wallet, displaying the gold detective badge.

She shrugged. "Lucky you. Here's what I have, Mr. Fernandez."

"Call me Frank."

"Okay, Frank. Our autopsy concluded death by strangulation. I took photographs of the odd-shaped ligature marks on the victim's neck to be able to prove in court that no bruising occurred during transportation of the body to our medical examiner's office. The autopsy showed interior damage to both carotid arteries, to the muscular tissue of the neck, and to the hyoid bone, which was crushed."

"It's strange," Fernandez said.

"The entire incident is eerie. You best be careful, Frank. Your investigation could lead to some dark places.

Fort Pierce is a Navy SEAL town. SEALs are instructed in strangulation techniques using wire with two sticks as handles. Once someone sets a garrote around a person's neck from behind, and has a clue as to what he's doing, he slices through the carotid arteries—there is no defense."

Fernandez could feel his insides beginning to tighten.

11

WORKING ON AN INVESTIGATION gave Frank Fernandez a renewed feeling of being needed, of doing something meaningful. He drove north on U.S. Route 1, past Taylor Creek Commons Shopping Center. Spotting Olsen Avenue, he checked for Halsey White's number and pulled into a gravel driveway.

No one answered the doorbell.

Fernandez heard a flinty voice. "Around back."

Halsey White was sitting in a screened-in porch. The captain had very tanned, wrinkled skin, a potbelly, gray fuzzy hair, and a beard, and he wore metal-framed eyeglasses. To Fernandez, Halsey White looked like an out-of-work mall Santa.

"State your business, young man."

"My name is Fernandez. Chief Brumberg asked me to look into the Campbell Lawrence case."

"Damn shame about Campbell." Halsey heaved a heavy sigh. "You could have called. Saved time. Would you like coffee? My daughter sent me one of them fancy new Keurig machines."

"I'm fine. Thank you."

"Who killed Campbell?"

"I'm sorry, sir. I can't get into the details of the case. I want to ask questions, but I can't really answer any from you."

"How about that?" Halsey said, folding his arms.

"I understand you're a treasure hunter?"

Halsey let the trace of a smile float across his face. He pushed the horn-rimmed glasses up his nose.

"People read Clive Cussler and think searching for hidden treasures hidden beneath the sea is exciting. What they don't realize are the days of stumbling on a pitching ship, fighting heavy seas, a churning stomach, and hours of back-breaking labor under a scorching sun."

Fernandez let the old man talk. He seemed lonely.

"Salvaging is an expensive hobby. You need a good boat, special equipment, and you got to pay and feed a crew—all that takes money." Halsey White chuckled. "But let me tell you something. It is also one of the most exciting adventures left on earth."

"Is that coffee offer still open?"

"How do you take yours?"

"Black, thanks."

When Halsey stood, Fernandez noticed he needed a cane to support himself.

"Damned spinal stenosis," Halsey grumbled.

Fernandez took the opportunity to phone Vesta. "Anything on the Lazarus Corporation?"

"I Googled. The Lazarus Corporation is the world's largest gold mining operation."

"Do me a favor. I interviewed the Ingram woman at the marina. Something didn't feel right. She may have been involved with the victim. Check her out and give me your impression."

AFTER HALSEY RETURNED, Frank cleared his throat. "Do you have any idea why anyone would want to harm Mr. Campbell? Did he ever speak about any group or individual being upset with him or holding a grudge?"

"No damn idea."

"You helped get him a slip at the marina. Can you tell me the nature of your relationship?"

Halsey shifted uncomfortably in his chair. "Campbell was studying shipwrecks. He wanted my input— everybody does. Every time I'm interviewed, half of Florida shows up in their little putt-putts, hunting for gold doubloons with their fancy metal detectors."

Fernandez's phone buzzed.

"Frank, you were going to keep in touch," Chief Brumberg growled. "The media is on my ass. What can I tell them?"

"Say the investigation is active and ongoing. Right now I'm with Halsey White."

He heard Brumberg sigh. "I've known Halsey for years. Not all bullshitters are treasure hunters, but all treasure hunters are bullshitters—Halsey is one of the best. He hit it big a few years back. Tell the grumpy bastard hello for me."

"Brumberg said you were a treasure hunter."

"You might say that. Let me show you something." Halsey hoisted himself painfully out of his chair and hobbled into the bedroom, returning with a newspaper.

FORT PIERCE TREASURE SALVAGER STRIKES GOLD

May 24, 2014: *Treasure Coast Press*

Fort Pierce resident Halsey White, 82, is a treasure hunter who uncovered gold—and a lot of it—off the coast of Fort Pierce. Peter Heller, owner of Crown Jewels LLC, the company that owns the rights to dive on the wreckage site, offered a conservative estimate of $275,000 for the gold necklace and ring recovered.

Heller's company bought the rights to the wreck site from the heirs of legendary treasure hunter Mel Fisher and allowed others, including Mr. White, to search under subcontracting agreements.

"To be the first person to touch an artifact in 300 years is indescribable," Halsey White said. "To dive beneath the sea and find and hold in your hand a weapon, a coin, a piece of jewelry, is an experience few people have. Fortunately, I have been one of those few people. I have seen the stuff that dreams are made of."

The centuries-old gold filigree necklace and ring were part of what has been identified as "The Queen's Jewels" from a Spanish treasure fleet struck by a strong hurricane off Florida's coast on July 30, 1715. More than 1,000 people were killed in the storm that claimed 11 of the dozen ships. Mounds of gold, silver and other artifacts were spilled across the ocean floor. Over the years, some were salvaged, but many treasure hunters and historians believe that millions of dollars in silver and gold still remain.

Under U.S. and Florida law, the treasure will be placed into the custody of the U.S. District Court in South Florida. The State of Florida will take possession of up to 20 percent of the find for display in a state museum. The rest will be split equally between Heller's company and Mr. Halsey White.

"VERY IMPRESSIVE," Fernandez said after glancing over the newspaper article. He opened his notebook. "What are the Queen's Jewels?"

"King Philip V of Spain lost his first wife and fetched himself a new bride. The Duchess of Parma agreed to marry Philip but refused to consummate the marriage until she got her dowry."

"No mon, no fun?"

Halsey ignored Fernandez's pun.

"The problem was that her dowry came from the king's colonies in the Americas and was being shipped aboard the 1715 Spanish plate fleet. The treasure convoy ran into a nasty hurricane and was wrecked."

Halsey grunted. "I can't remember my last bowel movement, but I sure recollect reading the old girl's dowry included emerald rings, 14-carat pearl earrings, a dragonhead gold ring, a long gold necklace, and a hell of a lot more."

"You found the necklace?"

He chuckled. "Gold is the devil's fishhook. I found both the necklace and the dragonhead ring."

"Were you alone?"

Halsey appeared not to hear the question.

"At that time I had a salvage boat, a small, wide-beamed converted fish trap boat built in the Keys. By mid-afternoon, I was tired and ready to quit. The wind had picked up to fifteen knots out of the east, pushing me toward the beach, so I decided to haul up the anchors and go home.

"My metal detector buzzed. It was an empty beer can. Then my metal detector buzzed again, and as I worked it back and forth over the sandy bottom, I got a hit. I kept the regulator in my mouth. Then I fanned through six to eight inches of sand with my fingers and spotted a long, butter-gold chain settled on the hard coral substrate under the sand.

"Onboard, I recognized it to be filigree gold. It weighed three pounds and was damn near 50 feet long. The chain had grains of sand imbedded in the links, so I was very careful unwinding it."

"How much was it worth?"

"Do you mean what did I net? Well, the necklace and ring sold at auction for $175,000. After Sotheby's deducted their commission, and the state of Florida took its 20 percent, and the lease owner got one half of the balance, and I paid taxes on my share, well, I'm not complaining, but I still need my Social Security to get by."

Fernandez could see the old captain was exhausted. "I'll tell you what," Halsey said in a hoarse voice. "She's still out there somewhere, covered by sand. Some days I can almost hear her whispering."

"Who is out there whispering?"

The old man seemed to nod off to sleep.

FRANK FERNANDEZ RETURNED to his office. Something stuck in his mind about the Halsey White interview, but it eluded him.

Vesta said, "I caught up with the girl from the marina before she left. The young woman is expecting."

"Expecting what?"

"Frank, maybe this is the right time for you to be winding down your career. Donna Ingram is pregnant."

...12

ON SATURDAY MORNING the Farmers' Market along the water's edge was bustling. Fernandez stopped for coffee at the Treasure Coast Coffee Traders tent. He sat on a bench overlooking the Indian River Lagoon, listening to the lapping sound of the sea against the rocks.

Seagulls and pelicans were strangely absent. Frank heard a hissing sound. He spotted a large, dark-colored bird circling over the water. It was the largest bird he had ever seen, with a wingspan of over ten feet. Must be a scavenger—a vulture, he thought.

The bird landed on one of the artificial reefs Fort Pierce had constructed in the Indian River Estuary. Frank noted the bird's glossy black plumage, powerful claws, and sharp, hooked beak. Then with a flutter, the massive bird lifted off, soaring on huge, motionless wings.

Fernandez crumpled his coffee cup, tossed it into a nearby trash container, and walked the short distance to the marina office.

Donna Ingram looked tearless and stoic.

"Can we talk?" he asked, realizing how lame that sounded. He was not looking forward to this interview, but the murder case had too much momentum to stop.

Donna seemed to sense his awkwardness. She dragged another chair into her office and closed the door. "I'd offer you coffee, but the smell makes me nauseous."

"No, I'm good. Thanks." He waited a moment and pressed on. "My assistant recounted her conversation with you—"

Donna Ingram nodded.

"When was the last time you saw your husband?" Frank waited for her response.

"Christmas."

"How would you describe your marriage?"

She dropped her eyes to the floor before speaking. "A lot of highs and lows."

"What is it now, high or low?"

Donna paused a long moment before opening her desk. She handed him a photo. "Excuse me, I have to use the bathroom."

The scowling guy in the snapshot looked fiercer and beefier than the smiling be-medaled young officer in her framed wedding picture. Jonas Ingram sported a reddish mustache and beard, sunglasses, and a dark green bandana on his head.

"Combat changes people," Donna said.

He saw the hard edge enter her eyes, the anger. "The Navy trains them to become warriors, to kill people, to lose close friends, see people blown up and maimed, and men like Jonas are expected not to come out with stress."

Fernandez didn't say anything. He knew that sometimes when he was quiet, the person he needed information from would eventually fill the silence.

"Between tours, my husband had trouble adjusting. When Jonas came home on leave, he would shut himself in the house and not want to go out. If we were driving somewhere, he would suddenly swerve to avoid trash or palm fronds in the road. He told me that in Iraq, road trash was used to hide bombs."

She sat quietly for a few moments. "I understand that a person couldn't go through all Jonas went through and not have problems. My husband definitely had his moods."

"Was he violent?"

"No. Jonas would never intentionally hurt me, but some nights he would wake up punching, or he would grab my arm. I was worried he could break it."

"Counseling was never discussed?"

"Are you serious? Counseling is frowned on by Navy SEALs. Their culture is 'Don't show signs of weakness.'"

Fernandez sensed a note of desperation in her voice.

"I felt that Jonas's SEAL teammates took precedence over me. In the last year, I felt shut out. And I have to say that after a while, I shut him out too."

Fernandez was silent.

"Women have needs. I was lonely. Jonas wasn't there for me when I needed him. He didn't have to volunteer for the last assignment."

"Where?"

"The Middle East somewhere."

Fernandez felt irritated listening to the woman bitch about her husband, but he kept his voice steady.

"Did you scuttle Lawrence's boat?"

"No."

"Do you know anyone with a motive to open the sea cocks and sink the boat?"

Donna shook her head.

He knew from her rapid eye blinks that she was lying.

"Was Campbell Lawrence the father of your child?"

She didn't respond.

Fernandez was painfully reminded of his own family situation and his failures as a husband. It put a catch in his throat.

"Did your husband know about your affair?"

"Fort Pierce is a small town."

"I understand how angry your husband would feel."

She stared, confused. "What are you talking about?"

Fernandez snapped his notebook shut. "Never mind."

…13

FRANK FERNANDEZ telephoned an old friend in Washington, senior FBI computer analyst Virginia Baker. Fernandez and Baker had had an on-and-off relationship when he was with the Bureau; a relationship of convenience between two agents grounded on sexual, not emotional, needs. Their liaisons were sporadic, usually weeks or months apart. Fernandez had been content to let Virginia be the one to initiate them.

She recognized his voice. "Hello, lover. I heard you retired to Florida. Did you start your chelation therapy?"

"Not yet."

He heard her inhale. "Frank, those bullet fragments in your chest could cause lead poisoning—"

"Maybe the bullets will work themselves out."

"You're impossible, Frank. Anyway, what can I do for you long distance?" In a throaty intonation she whispered, "I'd suggest phone sex, but the fools at NSA will listen in."

"Virginia, I need a favor."

"What are you doing chasing a case again?"

"I'm helping out the local police."

"Don't bullshit me, sweetheart. We both know why you're doing it. You miss the adrenaline rush."

"I'm tracing a Navy SEAL named Jonas Ingram. His SEAL team is stationed at Coronado, California. I need to know if the man traveled to Florida anytime around the end of July."

"Frank. If your guy's involved in an active SEAL operation, even the President would need to leap through hoops to track him down. This isn't *Saving Private Ryan.*"

"I'm not looking for restricted or classified information. I just need to know if Ingram was in Florida around the end of July."

He heard a deep intake of breath. "The SEALs are experts at avoiding detection. Maybe your man traveled under a fake ID, or hitched a ride on a military aircraft—"

He broke in. "Give it your best shot."

"Did I ever refuse you *anything,* honey?"

"IT'S SATURDAY, FRANK," Lou Brumberg groused. "I'm leaving the station in five minutes and taking my family to the Big Mouse in Orlando this weekend. Are you planning on spoiling it?"

"I think I've nailed your case. I need to run it by you."

Brumberg drummed a pencil on his desk.

"Donna Ingram's husband is my prime suspect."

"Jesus, Mary and Joseph!" Brumberg stammered.

"The Ingram woman is carrying Lawrence's kid."

"Are you insane?"

"Hear me out, Lou. In April, Campbell Lawrence brought his boat to Fort Pierce. He docked at the marina. Lawrence was a good-looking guy who liked the ladies. He put the moves on Mrs. Ingram. She's lonely and angry with her husband. Donna Ingram admits to having an affair with Lawrence—probably on his boat. Mrs. Ingram also implied Fort Pierce is a small town, a Navy SEAL town, home of the SEAL Museum, and someone might have seen her with Lawrence."

Lou Brumberg listened intently.

"My guess is Ingram got word of his wife's indiscretions and decided to take care of the situation himself. For SEALs, failure is not an option."

Brumberg struck the top of his desk with the palms of his hands and rose to his feet. "You think Jonas Ingram, who I've known since he was a pup, came back to Fort Pierce without anyone seeing him, strangled Lawrence, sunk his boat and poof—disappeared again?"

"Yes. I do. It's the holy trinity of crime: means, motive and opportunity. Ingram had the means: Navy SEALs are trained killers and the world's best underwater demolition experts. He surely had the motive: his wife was cuckolding him. And I believe I can prove he was in the area at the end of July."

Brumberg was red-faced. "You are off base. No DA would touch this with what you've got: no evidence, no weapon, no direct witness, no—"

The chief stopped as he thought of something. "Your personal family situation has clouded your vision. You saw what you wanted to see. You transferred your bitterness to Jonas Ingram. Any competent defense lawyer would deposition you about Maris and Maris's boy."

FERNANDEZ'S PHONE BUZZED and he checked the screen. The ID was Virginia Baker.

"Found your Navy SEAL, Frank."

"Fill me in."

"It's not pretty. Lieutenant Commander Ingram was part of a hostage rescue attempt last weekend that went sour in a Middle Eastern country. I would lose my pension if I told you where."

"Is Ingram alive?"

"Yes, but his injuries are serious. Commander Ingram was evacuated to the medical center in Landstuhl, Germany. The family is not being notified until the White House figures out how to spin it to the media."

Fernandez's cheeks felt hot. "Thank you, Virginia."

He put the phone down and stared at it for a few moments, wondering what his next move should or would be. He was drawing a blank.

"What's going on?" Brumberg asked.

Fernandez tried to think of something to say. He knew words were just words. It was every investigator's nightmare: a case bungled, allowing something dark and evil loose. His loneliness, anger and guilt had led him down the wrong path.

"Navy SEAL Jonas Ingram is in a hospital in Germany. I fucked up, Lou. I don't understand myself anymore. I don't know what the hell is happening to me." Frank added, "You want me off the case?"

The disdain in Brumberg's voice was unmistakable. "You can quit. You can limp along with self-pity, wondering why your holy trinity of detection failed, or you can man up, get the hell out of my office, and start earning your overpriced consultant fees."

PART TWO

NOSTROMO

...14

THE SKY TURNED from crimson to a fiery blood red band broken by the silhouettes of palm trees, their fronds rustling in the early morning breeze.

"Red sky in the morning," Halsey White mumbled. He understood if the morning sky turned fiery red, it meant a high water content in the atmosphere. Stormy weather was on its way.

Halsey thought he heard the front door opening.

"Around back," he yelled.

There was no answer.

"Who's there? Speak up, damn it."

The old man sensed something. Not a shadow, not even a sound, only a small movement behind him.

The first blow on Halsey's head disoriented him. He gasped. The walls were spinning.

The second crushing strike separated his brainstem from his spine. Halsey White crumpled to the floor.

Dark red blood filled his eyes. The blackness swam up and over Halsey White in waves. The old sea captain embarked upon a voyage to eternity. A strange silence descended.

The time was 06:47. The first drops of rain pattered against the windows. Stormy weather was on its way.

Red sky in morning, sailor takes warning.

...15

DAYLIGHT TRICKLED THROUGH the wood shutters. The phone call at 7:30 awakened Frank Fernandez from a fitful night's sleep.

Lou Brumberg sounded short of breath. "Halsey White has been murdered. Meet me at his house."

The Sunday morning traffic was light. Fernandez slowed when he saw patrol cars parked in front of Halsey White's gravel driveway. A uniformed officer held up the yellow crime scene tape to let him cross under.

Fernandez stood in the living room for a moment, taking in the bustle of activities involving forensic techs and police photographers. Miriam Jolson was ordering people about. She gave him a perfunctory wave.

He grimaced as he watched the forensic team slide Halsey's body onto a gurney and wheel it out the door.

"The victim was hit multiple times with a heavy club or a similar blunt instrument," Miriam Jolson said. "He was bludgeoned to death. We won't know for certain until the autopsy is performed Monday morning."

"Who discovered the body?" Fernandez asked.

Brumberg's face was ashen. "Halsey's next-door neighbor noticed the Sunday paper at the door. He knew the captain to be an early riser, so the guy checked. When no one answered the doorbell, he walked around to the back porch, found Halsey's body, and called us."

"Witnesses?"

"We canvassed all seven houses on the block. No one claimed to have seen or heard anything suspicious. The lack of damage to doors or windows indicated there was no break-in."

"Fingerprints?"

The chief shrugged. "Our people are dusting."

Fernandez took out his notebook. "Time of death?"

Jolson said, "I took Halsey's liver temperature and did the math. This isn't final, as you know, but I think around sunup."

"Is there a next of kin notification, Lou?"

"Halsey's daughter Ellie is flying in tonight, around midnight. It's Sunday and I'm shorthanded. Could you pick her up at the Palm Beach airport?"

Fernandez nodded.

Brumberg added, "Ellie can stay here if she wants to."

"Not a good idea, Lou. This is a crime scene. It might be a good idea to book his daughter a motel room."

Fernandez wanted to have a look around. He knew from experience that first impressions on a crime scene were important. Using plastic gloves, he flipped on the lights in Halsey's bedroom and spent a half hour going through drawers and closets without really knowing what he was looking for. He didn't find very much. What he did find surprised him. The dresser drawers appeared neatly arranged—too neatly arranged. He had the feeling that someone with a practiced hand had been through Halsey's clothes and put everything back in place.

In the bottom of a dresser drawer was a mahogany wooden box. Inside the satin-lined case he saw an assortment of military medals. The one that caught his eye was a Navy Cross, the second-highest military decoration for valor that can be awarded to a member of the United States Navy.

He moved the dresser away from the wall. Resting on the floor was a framed picture. The glass had cracked when the frame had fallen. It was an eight-by-ten black-and-white photograph, grainy and fading to a brownish yellow around the edges. In the picture were four men, all shirtless, all with dog tags taped together. Fernandez knew the men taped their tags to keep them from jangling when they were out on patrol. He snapped a picture with his digital camera.

Halsey's den was paneled in dark plywood. The room was tidy. The walls were lined with inexpensive reproductions of old wooden sailing ships.

On top of Halsey's desk was a photograph of an attractive young woman. In the center drawer Fernandez found the captain's black leather logbook. Skimming through the pages, everything seemed to be in order.

Fernandez felt a stab of uneasiness. His instincts told him something was out of place. He checked his notebook. Halsey had specified the date he'd located the Queen's Jewels was August 10. He searched for a log entry for that date. There was none. The page had been skillfully removed with a razor blade.

He called Brumberg. "Halsey's place has been turned —searched—and by pros. I can tell. They did a halfway decent job. There's something strange running through all of this, but I don't know what."

...16

IT WAS SUNDAY AFTERNOON. Fernandez went to his apartment to crash for a few hours before making the three-hour round trip to the airport. Halsey's daughter, Ellie, was scheduled to change planes in Atlanta and arrive in Palm Beach shortly after midnight.

His cell phone vibrated.

"Frank," Vesta said. "I saw Donna Ingram. A Navy SEAL officer had given her the bad news. I told her how proud we were of her husband. She was conflicted. Since she had flu symptoms, I suggested she wait a bit before traveling. It might be contagious."

"The flu?"

"Yes, dummy. The *flu*. I gave Donna the name of a doctor that could handle her *problem*. In a few weeks she will be well enough to fly to Germany to her husband's bedside. I hugged the girl, told her that my prayers were with her... and she gave me a backpack that belonged to Mr. Lawrence."

"Good work. Please leave it on my desk."

"Donna said she dropped Lawrence's computer and cell phone over the Indian River Bridge."

FRANK FERNANDEZ REPLAYED the Jonas Ingram scenario in his mind, regretting that he had built theories based upon pretzel logic. He could not put his finger on what was happening with the case, but he felt somehow things had shifted.

It had always been his practice to go back to the start whenever he hit a major snag. The start most often meant going back to the crime scene. But this case was different. He needed to see what was in Campbell Lawrence's backpack. He needed to push the case forward.

AN HOUR LATER, Fernandez was in his office, unloading Lawrence's backpack after forcing the latch. He had a half hour before he had to leave to pick up Halsey's daughter. On a legal pad he listed the contents of Lawrence's backpack.

(1) *Folder labeled: MAPS*
(1) *Folder labeled: DELGADO*
(1) *Folder labeled: H. WHITE*
(1) *Folder labeled: LAZARUS*
(1) *Diary labeled: PRIEST'S JOURNAL*
(1) *Passport*

Fernandez scanned the contents until he realized it was late. In a rush, he carried the backpack to his car and heaved it in the trunk. Lawrence's bag was heavier than he expected. He felt an uncomfortable tug in his upper body. Driving south on I-95, his chest started aching.

While with the Bureau, Fernandez had been wounded in a drug bust that went down badly. It involved the head of a drug cartel tipped off by an FBI insider. Fernandez had taken two rounds in the chest and nearly died. After he was released from the hospital, he'd hunted down and killed the informer.

Metal slivers remained in his chest, too close to the heart to be removed surgically. Despite the absence of symptoms, gunshot victims carrying lead bullet fragments in their bodies need to be aware of signs of lead poisoning—which are frequently fatal.

THE AMERICAN AIRLINES waiting area was deserted at midnight. Frank Fernandez found a comfortable seat. No coffee vendors were open at this hour. A few glum-looking travelers lugged their carry-on baggage into the arrival area.

From the photograph in Halsey's bedroom, he recognized Ellie St Clair. She looked tired, her mouth and eyes drawn.

Ellie St. Clair was an attractive woman in her early forties, a good decade or two younger than Fernandez. The grief was still holding in her eyes and at the corners of her mouth.

"Since no one else is here, you must be Fernandez."

"Please call me Frank."

"Thank you for meeting me at this ungodly hour."

"Do you have luggage we need to stop and pick up?"

"I travel light." Her eyes hardened. "This isn't a vacation."

Fernandez remained silent.

AFTER THEY EXITED THE AIRPORT ramp on to I-95, Ellie St. Clair said, "I presume you are connected to the police."

"That's right."

"I couldn't process what Lou Brumberg was babbling on the phone. I was in shock. Halsey was in good health for his age." Her voice trembled. "I'm a psychotherapist and I counsel other people, but when it's your own..." She hesitated. "How could this happen? It's monstrous."

"I am very sorry to have to tell you this, ma'am."

"Don't call me 'ma'am.' I'm not your mother."

Fernandez's face flushed. He drove for a few minutes in silence, trying to maintain a professional presence.

"How did it happen? I have a right to know."

"Your father was bludgeoned. We're not sure who did it."

He heard her sharp intake of breath.

"Oh, my God," she said, bringing one hand to her mouth. She seemed to be withdrawing into herself.

They drove in silence.

Passing the Jupiter exit, Ellie grumbled, "I grew up around here. Stop on Bridge Road and U.S. 1 at the gas station. I need a restroom and coffee."

ELLIE ST. CLAIR SIPPED her steaming coffee. "It's my job to counsel others." Her lips tightened again. "But when it's your own parent…"

Fernandez didn't interrupt.

"Are you a detective?" she asked.

"Something like that, yeah."

She raised a quizzical eye at his answer.

"Actually, I'm a state-licensed private investigator. But I was an FBI agent for almost twenty years. The Fort Pierce police were shorthanded, and there was a hiring freeze because of budget cuts. I was retained as a consultant on this case."

"Are you trying to be funny? Budget cuts? You're a goddamn rent-a-cop; this is unbelievable."

Fernandez grunted. Her comment didn't merit an answer. He shrugged, retreating into silence.

She put her head against the window and nodded off.

When Fernandez pulled into the Hutchinson Island Inn parking lot, Ellie St. Clair awoke, rubbed her stiff neck, grabbed her carry-on, got out, and without a word, slammed the car door.

"You're welcome," Fernandez mumbled.

...18

THE PHONE CALL woke Frank Fernandez. He managed to push the right button on the second try and said something that vaguely resembled hello.

"I wanted to thank you for meeting me at the airport," Ellie St. Clair said, "and to apologize for my boorish behavior. Yesterday was a long and tough day. Sorry."

Fernandez paused to collect his thoughts. He wondered, *Why the turn-around?* Instinctively he knew. "You backgrounded me. How did you manage that?"

"One of my patient's husband is with the FBI in Monterrey. I e-mailed him. He didn't know you personally, but according to FBI scuttlebutt, you're kind of a legend."

"I don't know about that."

"He said you could have had the job of FBI Director but turned it down."

"Too many strings attached. I wouldn't satisfy the gods of political expediency."

"Why did they call you St. Fernandez?"

"Long story. Have you had breakfast?"

"No."

"I'll pick you up in a half-hour."

"Lovely. I'm going back to Carmel earlier than expected.

"Why?"

"Also a long story." She hung up.

"IN THE WINTER YOU STAND IN LINE because this place is so busy," Frank said. He motioned to the waitress to seat them overlooking the Fort Pierce Inlet. Gentle ocean winds fanned the palm trees. They sat quietly, watching herring gulls swoop low over the mouth of the inlet.

In an instant the gulls were gone. The only sound they heard was the rhythmic crashing and sucking of the water against the jetty rocks.

"My gosh," Ellie said, pointing. "That's what frightened off the birds: it's a condor."

To Fernandez, it appeared to be the same large bird he had seen circling over the water at the Farmers' Market on Saturday morning. "I thought it was a vulture."

"The species are related. It's rare to see a condor in Florida. That is the largest I've ever seen. She must be an Andean condor."

"She?"

"Male Andean condors have white patches on their wings, large fleshy lumps on the front of their heads, and neck wattles that are absent in females."

Their waitress took their orders. "Two breakfast specials," Frank said.

"Hash browns or home fries, honey?"

Ellie St. Clair coughed deeply and shook her head. "Fruit for me, thanks."

Nasty cough, Fernandez thought.

"HOW DO YOU KNOW about condors?"

"They fascinate me. The condor is one of the largest birds in the world. They nest mainly in California on our

Monterrey Peninsula and in South America, in the Peruvian Andes."

Fernandez remained silent.

"I know. I'm avoiding talking about Halsey."

"I met your dad. We talked for over an hour."

"Did he bend your ear about the Golden Madonna?"

"It was never mentioned."

She narrowed her eyes. "You're joking."

Fernandez shook his head.

"How odd. What *did* Halsey talk about?"

"Finding pieces of the Queen's Jewelry."

Ellie coughed again into her handkerchief. Her body language indicated frustration. "That's not possible. The Golden Madonna was all Halsey ever talked about. All he lived for—"

Frank held up his hands. "Humor me, please. What's the Golden Madonna?"

Irritation crept into her voice. "My father was preoccupied with salvaging gold from sunken ships. His obsession took priority over… everything else. After my mother died, my father went to Spain. The trip was an extravagance he could ill afford."

Ellie hesitated. Her face stiffened. "After his trip to Spain, Halsey changed. The Golden Madonna became an obsession. Halsey believed King Philip IV ordered a life-sized statue of the Virgin Mary to be cast in the purest gold found in Peru. The icon was to be shipped to Spain aboard the galleon *Maravillas*.

"It sounds hokey, but Halsey said the king believed if he offered something of great value to the church, in return God would protect his treasure ships."

"What's unusual about that? Every day television ministry hawkers ask viewers to send in money to the church."

She ignored his remark.

"My father told me that according to Spanish documents, the *Maravillas* sailed from Havana in 1656. Aboard were 5 million pesos of treasure and a gold edifice wrapped in lamb's wool."

"More coffee?" the waitress interrupted.

They both nodded.

Fernandez listened, fascinated.

"The ship hit a sandbar on the uncharted shoals of Los Mimbres off Little Bahama Bank. A few people survived; the rest were swept to sea or eaten by sharks."

"That's a pleasant image."

"This Golden Madonna had fastened herself on my father's mind. Halsey became obsessed. He spent years and money salvaging, until the Bahamian government stopped granting leases on the wreck site.

"Halsey's wish was to have his ashes placed in an urn and buried on the site of the *Maravillas*. He had obtained permission from the Bahamian government."

"What changed the plans?"

Ellie St. Clair offered a wan smile. "Last month I received a note from Halsey's lawyer with a codicil to his will. For some peculiar reason, Halsey changed his mind. He wanted his ashes dropped at the site where he salvaged the Queen's Jewels." Ellie shook her head. "It makes no sense at all." She paused. "It was like the dog that didn't bark."

"I don't follow you."

"One of the Sherlock Holmes stories concerned the disappearance of a race horse and on the murder of its trainer. A Scotland Yard detective asked Holmes for his opinion. Holmes referred to the 'curious incident of the dog in the night-time.' The detective said, 'The dog did nothing in the night-time.' Holmes replied, 'That was the curious incident.'"

Fernandez understood Ellie was trying to tell him something important. What it was, he had no idea.

"IT"S YOUR TURN. Why did they call you a saint?"

Fernandez took a long pull on his coffee. He let his shoulders droop. "In the good-old-boy FBI network of ex-jocks and frat boys, loyalty trumps truth."

Ellie raised her eyebrows.

"In 1993, the Bureau of Alcohol, Tobacco and Firearms bungled a raid on a dissident religious group near Waco, Texas. Their leader, David Koresh, threatened an apocalypse if federal agents entered his Branch Davidian compound. The FBI and the Army mounted a fifty-one-day siege. According to official FBI documents, Koresh's people ignited a suicidal pyre. In the inferno, 74 men, women and children died—including twelve kids under five years old."

Ellie shuddered involuntarily.

"A few years later, I was working in the FBI warehouse in Quantico. I spotted some boxes with no markings. Out of curiosity, I opened them and found tapes and documents relating to the 1993 Waco incident. It surprised me, because FBI officials had sworn in court that such evidence did not exist.

"The first document I read reported that on April

19th, Army tanks had rammed holes in the main Branch Davidian compound and pumped CS gas into the structures. CS gas is a riot control agent."

Fernandez pushed back his coffee. "The buildings were saturated with the CS gas and spilled kerosene. Around noon, two military pyrotechnic devices were fired into the main building. Those flash-producing projectiles sparked the fire that engulfed the complex in flames and—"

He paused. "Waco fire department trucks were prevented by the FBI from approaching the inferno. To make matters worse, the burned-out ruin was razed in an attempt to remove evidence."

"What did you do?"

"I telephoned FBI director Bill Glenner. He dispatched a team to take possession of the four boxes. Glenner contacted the attorney general. She called a press conference and conceded that after years of denials, pyrotechnic tear gas canisters had, in fact, been used at the Branch Davidian compound. The attorney general implied that the FBI had misled her. The public exposure caused embarrassment and ruffled feelings throughout the Bureau. Somehow I was named as the whistle blower, the virtuous, but disloyal team player, ergo: Saint Fernandez."

THEY SAT IN THE CAR outside the restaurant. "If you could give me a few more minutes?"

She nodded agreement.

"Did Halsey have any enemies?"

"Not that I know of."

Fernandez opened his iPhone and showed Ellie the photo he had taken at Halsey's home. "Do you know any of these men?"

"That's Dad, of course, with his crew. He was a first class petty officer serving as PBR boat captain."

"What's a PBR?"

"Patrol Boats River in the Vietnam War." She squinted. "The big man on the right looks like Ossie Williams. Ossie sometimes salvaged with Halsey."

Fernandez jotted down his name.

"Any others?"

"No. This photo was taken before I was born."

"What was Halsey's relationship with Lawrence?"

"I have no idea."

Fernandez felt a tickle of nervousness. "How about dinner? I know where they serve the best key lime pie."

For the first time she smiled. "I love key lime pie."

His phone buzzed.

"Where the hell are you?" Lou Brumberg grumbled on the phone. "You have got to keep me in the loop. The mayor called a press conference for 12:00. It's important. Be there!"

...19

BY NOON, THE TEMPERATURE had risen into the mid-nineties. The Fort Pierce police station was a boxy, one-story brown building with a patch of satellite dishes and antenna sprouting from the roof. With no offshore breeze, pennants drooped on the flagpole.

A small herd of media crowded into the conference room. Mayor Westlake stood behind a podium, looking over the audience. Police Chief Louis Brumberg, in full uniform, was by his side. Several reporters were standing. There wasn't enough seating for everyone. It was noisy.

Frank Fernandez entered, perspiring. He positioned himself with his back to the wall between those who would ask questions and those who would answer them.

Mayor Westlake rapped lightly on the microphone with his pen. The mayor was a tall, well-built African-American man with a mop of white hair.

With a practiced smile, Westlake said, "I am pleased to see so many members of the media attending this press conference. As you all know, this case is receiving national attention, which could have a disruptive impact on tourism and local business."

There was a mutter of disapproval at his remarks.

Westlake handed the microphone to Brumberg.

"My name is Chief Louis Brumberg. I'll make some preliminary remarks and then try to answer your questions. As you know from newspaper reports, a man's body was found a mile offshore Bathtub Beach in Stuart. The victim's name is Campbell Lawrence from Key West,

Florida. As far as we know, Mr. Lawrence had no living relatives."

Brumberg paused to open a folder. "Yesterday morning we were called to the scene of another homicide. The victim was Captain Halsey White, a resident of Fort Pierce. Captain White is survived by a daughter."

With that remark, Brumberg asked for questions.

Hands were raised.

Fernandez studied the people in the room. One lady he recognized, Alise Smith, had worked for the *New York Times* before retiring to Fort Pierce to handle special assignments for the local paper.

Question: "What were the times of death?"

Answer: "Lawrence's death occurred at 6:44 Thursday, and Captain Halsey White died at 6:47 Sunday."

Question: "Do you know who committed the murders?"

Answer: "Not yet, unfortunately."

Question: "Why were these two men singled out?"

Brumberg shook his head. "No idea."

Alise Smith asked, "Wasn't Halsey White the man who salvaged gold jewelry from a Spanish treasure ship?"

Answer: "That is correct."

Follow up question: "Are the murders connected in any way to sunken treasure?"

Answer: "Not as far as we know."

Question: "Have you any leads?"

Answer: "The investigation is still in process."

Question: "Was the boat sinking sabotage?"

Answer: "Mr. Lawrence's boat was under water for several days, so the chance of retrieving forensic evidence is slight."

Question: "Are you looking for a serial killer?"

After an awkward pause: "It's too early to speculate."

Alise Smith asked another question. "Chief Brumberg, in your opinion, is the lack of progress due to budget cuts resulting in insufficient police staffing?"

Mayor Westlake surprised Brumberg by retaking the microphone.

"Ms. Smith, our city administration is proactive. The Federal Bureau of Investigation has been notified of the crime committed in waters off of Hutchinson Island. Their agents will arrive midweek to handle the investigation."

Brumberg gawked in surprise.

Fernandez felt a surge of dismay.

The crowd scattered as the press conference ended.

Alise Smith placed her hand lightly on Frank's shoulder. "Do you know anything at all?"

He shook his head.

The mayor was standing by the podium.

"Mr. Fernandez," he said. "Your consulting services are no longer required."

"IT'S A GIANT RAT FUCK," Brumberg groused after Westlake left. "Calling in the FBI takes the monkey off his shoulder. The fact that the Coast Guard found Lawrence's body offshore makes it legit. And if the Bureau gets involved, the expenses won't impact Westlake's budget. Uncle Sugar will pick up the tab."

Fernandez nodded. It made a certain amount of sense.

"I'm sorry, Frank. Forty-eight hours and then your old chums take over."

LEARNING THAT THE FBI was taking over the case roiled Frank Fernandez. Years before, his flashes of inspiration had provided solutions to difficult cases; now he had no more bright ideas. He sat in silence, thinking. Time was running out; forty-eight hours and he was off the case. He made a mug of steaming black coffee. Campbell Lawrence's property was evidence and would have to be turned over to the FBI.

He emptied Lawrence's backpack, arranging the contents in chronological order.

DELGADO
A PRIEST'S JOURNEY
H. WHITE
PASSPORT
LAZARUS
MAPS

Lawrence's initial correspondence was dated October 2013.

THE GOLDEN MADONNA

Directorate General of Cultural Heritage
Ministry of Culture
Plaza del Rey 1
Madrid, Spain 28004

October 12, 2013
Re: *Nuestra Senora de las Maravillas*

Dear Sirs:

I am a salvager operating out of Key West, Florida. As you are no doubt aware, the *Maravillas* sunk in 1656 off Grand Bahamas Island, filled with over five million pesos of treasure.

Your Spanish salvagers recovered almost half a million pesos. The Bahamian government has not granted leases on the *Maravillas* site since 1990. With the legal ruling in the Odyssey Marine Exploration case, the Bahamian government is now expected to relax its restrictions, which brings me to the purpose of this letter.

I am interested in undertaking a salvage exploration of the *Maravillas*. This requires securing investment capital. In light of the Odyssey decision, would your government be willing to finance my undertaking? I can provide references and cost estimates for the salvaging project.

I propose an arrangement whereby I receive ten percent of the assessed value of the recovered cargo. Spain would cover the salvaging costs and receive 90 percent of the assessed value.

Looking forward to your reply.

Yours truly,
Campbell Lawrence

December 15, 2013
Dear Mr. Campbell Lawrence:

Your correspondence has been forwarded to my attention. We were pleased with the Odyssey ruling. Spain is aware of the treasure resting on the ocean floor off the Florida coastline.

Government regulations prohibit the pre-funding of salvage explorations of ships wrecked centuries ago. However, should your efforts prove fruitful in recovering artifacts and should Spain be awarded legal custody, we would agree to remit to you 10 percent of the current appraised value.

If there are ways we may be of assistance, please do not hesitate to contact us by letter, facsimile: 34-91-522-9305 or e-mail address: carlos.delgado@mcu.es.

I wish you well in your venture.

Cordially,
Carlos Delgado
Director General
Cultural Heritage
Ministry of Culture

Email: carlos.delgado@mcu.es
CAMPBELL LAWRENCE
To: Carlos Delgado
February 7, 2014

Dear Señor Delgado:
Whatever documentation you can make available referencing 'unlisted' manifest items

shipped on the *Maravillas* will be appreciated; in particular a religious icon, a Golden Madonna.

    Thank you,
    Campbell Lawrence

Email Reply: c.lawrence@aol.com
MINISTRY OF CULTURE
To: Campbell Lawrence
February 10, 2014

My Dear Lawrence,
Re: Golden Icon:
Forwarding priest's journal.
Good luck.
Carlos

Email: carlos.delgado@mcu.es
CAMPBELL LAWRENCE
To: Carlos Delgado
Ministry of Culture
April 6, 2014

Dear Carlos:
Thank you for Badrena's journal.
Focus shifting to 1715 Treasure Fleet.
Thanks
Campbell

On a yellow pad Fernandez noted that Campbell Lawrence became interested in salvaging the Spanish treasure galleon *Maravillas* in 2013 after a legal ruling would likely cause the Bahamian salvage ban to be lifted.

This would give Spain legal custody of gold and artifacts recovered by salvors.

The Spanish were not prepared to up-front money, but they agreed to pay him a consideration if Lawrence proved successful. Because of the favorable Odyssey ruling, the Spanish were forthcoming with information and documentation.

Something gnawed at Fernandez. He wasn't able to grasp it; maybe it would float to the surface if he stopped putting pressure on himself.

On or about April 2014, after Lawrence received the priest's journal, he had lost interest in the *Maravillas* and turned his attention to the 1715 fleet. Why? It was difficult to explain.

He gazed out the window at Indian River Drive. An elderly woman walked her small white shih tzu.

Ellie told him Halsey White also had lost interest in the *Maravillas*. She said it was impossible to explain. Fernandez wondered, *Is this another dog that didn't bark?*

ARCHIE'S SEABREEZE WAS A RUSTIC, iconic, run-down-looking Florida beach restaurant located across A1A from the Atlantic Ocean. Archie's anchored the bar scene on Hutchinson Island, drawing a mix of bikers, tourists, locals and retirees. At 8 p.m. the atmosphere was pure buzz, with a tuneful backdrop of live music from a solo balladeer.

Frank Fernandez and Ellie St. Clair were seated at an outside table, watching the fading rays of sunlight. Evening was coming full on, and with it the mosquitoes.

They ordered a pitcher of beer and studied the menu.

"On Sundays they hold church services here."

She eyed him suspiciously.

He drank off half his beer. "Your father told me that the search for hidden treasures under the sea was one of the most exciting adventures left on earth."

"That's my *Nostromo*." Her smile was gone. "Did you ever read Joseph Conrad?"

"Maybe in college. I don't remember."

"Joseph Conrad wrote a novel called *Nostromo* set in a mythical South American republic. The protagonist is Nostromo, a stevedore, a man of honesty and integrity. In the plot, Nostromo was assigned the dangerous task of taking a large amount of silver to sea to save it from falling into the hands of revolutionaries. When Nostromo finally returned, everyone thought his boat and silver had sunk, and no one appreciated his brave deed. The man decided to keep the silver. He became obsessed with the treasure. Drained of integrity and nobility, Nostromo began to unravel. Finally, just before Nostromo's death, Joseph Conrad explains the cause of his downfall.

> *There is something in a treasure that fastens upon a man's mind. He will curse the day he ever heard of it, and will let his last hour come upon him, still believing that he missed it only by a foot. He will never forget it until he is dead, and even then there is no getting away from a treasure that once fastens on your mind.*

"How can you remember such a long quote?"

"It should be Halsey White's eulogy."

The waitress came up with another pitcher of beer.

"Did you have a good relationship with Halsey?"

She looked at him over a glass of wine. The wrinkle at the corner of her mouth deepened. "We were at odds for a while. Halsey didn't trust my husband. In retrospect, I don't blame him. Martin was a lawyer. He went to law school in Florida—that's how we met. His family lived in Albuquerque, so we settled there. I worked as a psychiatric therapist with the VA. After ten years of a so-so marriage, Martin emptied our bank account and marched off into the sunset… with a younger woman."

Fernandez refilled her glass from the pitcher.

She took in a deep breath. "I'm supposed to be able to handle crisis; I'm a psychiatric therapist, right?"

He didn't respond.

"Wrong. I had the full-blown fall-aparts: the guilt, embarrassment, shame and financial worries; all the baggage I help others deal with." Ellie emptied her glass. "Halsey helped me emotionally."

A wintry smile touched the sides of her mouth. "He told me I was a gifted therapist, and while talent was a wonderful thing, it wouldn't carry a quitter." She paused. "So I moved on, to Carmel, and opened my own practice."

Fernandez looked down at his beer mug. He had met this woman less than 24 hours ago, yet he couldn't deny his attraction to her. He didn't know what to say.

Ellie interrupted his thoughts. "At first I had trouble making friends. I know from my experience with clients that discarded wives, especially those with no children, often suffer from undeserved feelings of being unloved and unattractive."

"You are too beautiful to feel that way." He knew his remark embarrassed her. "Sorry."

Ellie smiled. "No. No, that was nice. Thank you."

Fernandez felt sudden warmth in his groin.

Now we are flirting, he thought. A deliberate mention of an ex-husband had to count as flirting. Though he wasn't certain. He hadn't flirted in a while.

They sat talking for nearly an hour after the food was gone. She asked about his life and his reason for joining the FBI. It was more than curiosity.

"After my discharge from the Marines, I was encouraged by my closest friend to join the Bureau. I believed it was important Hispanics be represented in the Bureau."

"What did your parents say?"

"My mother didn't say anything. She died before I finished high school."

"What about your father?"

"As a young man my father worked crops in California. He picked strawberries. Dad volunteered for the Army during the Korean War and went to college on the G.I Bill. He became a pharmacist. After Mother's death, he remarried, started a new family. He works part time. We've lost touch."

"Why?"

"My father preached to me and my brother that as a minority, we needed a profession. He distrusted politicians. 'With a profession,' he said, 'if you're persecuted, you can move anywhere and take your profession with you.' I was a rebel. My father was furious when I joined the FBI. Looking back, he made good sense. My brother is a doctor. I'm fifty-five and know nothing except law enforcement and criminal investigations. All I'm qualified for is working in the security business."

"Did you regret joining the FBI? Didn't you ever feel you were helping people?"

"Sometimes, but not always."

He sensed something important rode on what he told her. She was making a decision about him.

"My life is complicated. At the moment I'm content handling one thing at a time."

Ellie reached across and touched his hand. "Saying 'It's complicated' is a common answer people give when it's not convenient for them to face reality. I might be able to help you."

"Thanks. But I don't know you well enough—"

She broke in. "That's another stall. Try me?"

Fernandez felt a connection between them. Her words "Try me" had multiple interpretations. The beers loosened his tongue.

"I was cuckolded by my wife."

Ellie squeezed his hand. "You must have feelings of bitterness and anger," she said. "Do you know 33 percent of all men and 19 percent of women admit to cheating on their spouses? And those statistics are low; most people avoid telling the truth."

"Are your statistics supposed to make me feel better?"

"Were you 100 percent faithful to your wife?"

He reddened but was quiet.

Fernandez's phone buzzed; it was Brumberg. He ignored it.

Ellie continued. "Men tend to forgive themselves for their indiscretions, but they find it much harder to forgive their wives. For a betrayed woman, an affair is an offense against her dignity. For a betrayed man, it's an offense against his manhood. It goes right to the core of his identity. It makes him feel *weak*."

"That's not the whole problem."

"What's the *whole* problem? Do you have cancer?"

"No. I have a son—and he's not mine. My wife was a museum director who lost her job in Fort Pierce. I should have been suspicious when she immediately landed a position with the Dali Museum in Sarasota, and then told me she was pregnant. Now she's living with the guy and wants a divorce."

Ellie listened quietly before speaking. "Your situation is difficult, but not as uncommon as you might imagine. Children like yours, born as a result of unplanned circumstances, are sometimes cruelly labeled ghost children—and treated that way. Life isn't fair. My mother died of heart disease when I was six."

Her comments gave him pause. He drained his glass, waiting for her to finish.

"There is a kid in Sarasota who might, just might, be fortunate enough to have two caring fathers."

A shiver ran through him. "I'm not ready for that—"

She broke in. "We could work on that, but now I really need to get going."

AT THE MOTEL ENTRANCE Ellie placed her hand on Frank's shoulder. Then she moved her body close, pressing her breasts against him.

"Halsey's ashes won't be released for a few days. Since he was a holder of the Navy Cross, the SEALs will handle the scattering of his ashes. I'm going back to California tomorrow. Come and visit."

Fernandez grimaced.

"I hope I didn't scare you away with that invitation."

"There's a ten-year age difference between us."

"I'm not asking you to marry me."

"Do you need help packing and shipping any of your dad's... stuff?"

"No. Thanks. Most is leased or junk. I called Treasure Coast Hospice. They will dispose of everything."

A tear trickled down her cheek. She slapped it away with the heel of her hand.

They stared at each other. Then she moved closer and brought her mouth up to his. She kissed his cheek, which was scratchy; he hadn't shaved that morning.

She pressed herself against him in a way that revealed her need. He saw her eyes were closed, and in that moment he realized she echoed his loneliness.

"It's been a long time for me," she whispered. "Would you like to—"

"Yes," he said without hesitation.

THEY KISSED LIGHTLY. No words were necessary. Ellie pulled away and flicked off the lights. Moonlight glimmered off the water of the Fort Pierce Inlet. Her milky white skin shone in the semi-darkness.

Frank stepped closer to her and touched her. He looked at her face and saw worry behind her eyes, determination in the set of her jaw. With a hint of concern in his voice, he said, "Are you okay with this?"

"All I want is this moment. It's all we have."

They undressed each other slowly. Fernandez stood naked at the foot of the bed for a few minutes, and they smiled at each other. Ellie looked beautiful to him. She was thin, almost girlish, with small breasts and a small, flat stomach.

When he climbed onto the bed next to her, Ellie ran her fingers over the twin welts of pinkish scar tissue. She brushed her mouth against his chest. "How did you get the scars?"

Fernandez pressed his thumb and forefinger to the bridge of his nose, trying to block the unsettling force dragging his mind back in time: hearing the gun roar, feeling the searing heat as the two bullets lodged in his chest, fracturing his ribs, puncturing his lung; warm blood inside his shirt; struggling against the pain; the blackness swimming over him in waves until he passed out.

He took a deep breath. "I was agent in charge of an FBI raid in Florida. Our mission was to arrest a Colombian drug lord. The man was making a rare visit to the U.S., and we had a solid-gold insider tip. He was scheduled to supervise a cocaine transaction worth millions. The drug bust came up empty. Someone tipped them off, and I was shot."

"Were the bullets removed?"

He shook his head. "Too many fragments—less than a centimeter from my heart. I don't think much about it anymore. They're just a part of me, embedded in the muscle. The doctors say it would cause more damage going in to remove them."

He rolled onto her and kissed her deeply. *I love you,* he thought but didn't say.

Ellie positioned herself on top. She was very silent, her movements steady and gentle, her face above him breathing in short gasps. A teardrop hit his cheek.

Later he whispered, "It's been a long time for me too."

She put one hand on Frank's face, feeling in the dark as if she were a blind woman. "I know. You were a little rusty—the first time."

Something strange had occurred, an intimacy that Frank had never experienced before.

"You will come to Carmel?" Ellie asked.

"I promise. I really promise."

She smiled and shook his hand. "Deal."

Fernandez wished with all his heart that he could have kept that promise to Ellie St. Clair, but it was a promise he would never keep.

...21

IT WAS LATE WHEN FRANK Fernandez returned home. The idea of moving to Carmel, California, appealed to him. His feelings for Ellie St. Clair were deeper than passion. He didn't want to live alone the rest of his life. With FBI credentials, he could be a plain-vanilla private detective and get plenty of work.

He made a mug of steaming black coffee. The FBI was due in a day or two. Time was running out. The case was slipping away from him. He used to be able to sniff out clues, find the flaws. A wave of melancholy swept over Frank. He realized it had been a mistake taking on this assignment.

What did Halsey tell his daughter? "Talent is a wonderful thing, but it won't carry a quitter."

Fernandez picked up the translated chronicle entitled *A Priest's Journal*, written by Father Don Manuel de Badrena.

PART III

THE PRIEST'S JOURNAL

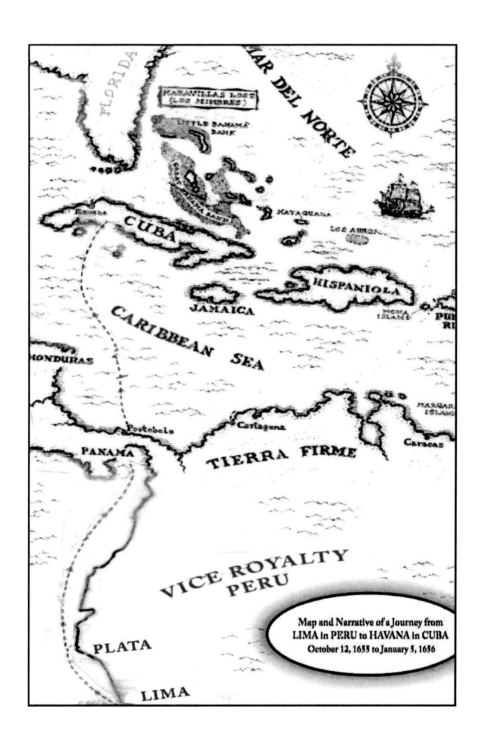

Map and Narrative of a Journey from
LIMA in PERU to HAVANA in CUBA
October 12, 1655 to January 5, 1656

...22

A JOURNAL

Faithfully related by the person concerned therein,

Don Manuel de Badrena

I would not dare to put in your hands the following story were it not true. For fifteen years, I served as a cleric at the Cathedral of Lima, the church officially inaugurated by Francisco Pizarro on March 11, 1540.

My responsibilities included daily recitation of the Liturgy of the Hours, ministering the Sacrament of Penance and the Anointing of the Sick. The clergy assigned to the churches in Lima did not travel excessively. Life was pleasant, especially compared to distant outposts in the cold and mountainous ranges of Chile, or the disease-plagued assignments in Panama.

In the late summer of 1655, the Council of the Indies notified Viceroy Don Garcia de Guzman that a priest's service was required for a certain ecclesiastic mission. When I was selected, I felt it was the first time in years something positive was happening on my behalf.

Together with two soldier-guards, I was assigned to shepherd a full-size solid-gold statue of the Virgin Mary holding the Christ Child. This sacred relic was to be safely transported from Lima to Panama, thence by boat to Havana and finally home to the Cathedral in Seville. The icon was encased in an eight-foot wooden box stored in the stern castle cabin next to the captain's. My two soldier-guards occupied the cabin with the sacred relic.

In addition, while on board ship I was instructed to conduct prayers of the Santisimo Sacramento to be sung every Thursday and the Purisima Conception every Saturday. I also agreed to tend to soldiers and seamen becoming ill during the voyage, as there was not an official physician on board.

ON THE TWELFTH DAY of the tenth month October 1655, the Armada de Mar de Sur, consisting of three galleons, sailed from the Peruvian port of Callao, groaning under the weight of treasure stowed in their holds. I was a passenger on the *Nuestra Senora de la Dasso*, a treasure galleon under the command of Captain Bartolomé de Navarro. The ship's nine sails filled from a swift easterly offshore breeze that pushed her 570-ton bulk through the rolling swells at a comfortable five knots.

We left Callao bound for Panama, where my sacred cargo would be packed aboard mules for a journey across the isthmus to Port Bello, then loaded aboard a galleon to set sail for Havana and then across the Atlantic to Spain.

According to Captain Navarro, he intended to sail north along the rugged South American coast 515 nautical miles to Paita. From there he would head seaward to avoid the dangerous promontory of Santa Elena, and then to Perico, the Port of Panama.

THE FIFTEENTH DAY of the tenth month of October. Pushed by a balmy and moderate breeze from the south-southwest, and aided by a three-knot current, our ship was making excellent headway. Just before sunset one evening, my cabin mate, Gonzalo del Campo, related a fascinating tale.

Del Campo was a sixty-year-old former Spanish soldier. His army service over, Campo settled down and married an Indian girl. After her recent death, he wished to return to his birthplace, Cadiz. Like many soldiers posted to the New World, Gonzalo had never practiced religion or received sacraments.

My new friend was much taken with the prospect of salvation. For that reason, I judge the story related to me to be true as he was led to understand it from his wife's grandfather, a witness to the perfidious murder of the Inca king Atahualpa.

Gonzalo's words confounded me, as I had hitherto believed Francisco Pizarro to be the noblest of Spanish adventurers. I found the story of Pizarro's greed so improbable that I paid little attention.

According to Gonzalo's story, in 1533 Pizarro came to the Inca capital of Cajamarca accompanied by 168 conquistadors—62 on horse, the rest on foot. He captured the Inca king Atahualpa. The

Inca ruler considered it inconceivable that a small party of foreigners, isolated and far from home, could pose a threat to him. In addition, Atahualpa was fascinated with reports of the bearded white men's horses—an animal unknown to the Incas.

"What happened next," Gonzalo related, "was extraordinary. Instead of ordering his army to attack the Spanish, Atahualpa struck a deal. Knowing the Spaniard's greed for gold, he stood on his tiptoes, reached his hand as high as the wall of the room, and promised Pizarro that in return for his freedom, he would fill his cell with gold to the height of the line and 'twice as much silver, besides.'

"I've been inside that room," Gonzalo added. "It measures seventy by twenty-two feet, and the mark is eight feet from the floor."

The old soldier broke off from his remembering. His face was red with indignation. "Atahualpa believed all the gold being collected would satisfy Pizarro, but he was wrong. Pizarro's greed was limitless."

I pleaded with the man to proceed.

"On July 26, Pizarro reneged on his promise to Atahualpa and condemned him to be burned at the stake in the city square of Cajamarca. There was no trial, nothing but a panicky decision by Pizarro."

"How ghastly," I said.

"Wait. It gets worse. Atahualpa was horrified at the thought of being burned alive, not so much because of the physical pain, but because it would mean the destruction of his body. The Incas believed the corpse must be intact for the dead to live in the next world. As an Inca, Atahualpa's mummy would be venerated by his lineage."

Gonzalo looked vexed. "Your Catholic church offered Atahualpa a sham conversion to Christianity to preserve his body. The Inca chief agreed, whereby he was forthwith garroted by a piece of rope that was tied around his neck. No sooner had Atahualpa been strangled than Pizarro reneged again, burned Atahualpa's corpse, and had his ashes interred in the new church of San Francisco in Cajamarca."

As soon as Pizarro left for Cuzco, Gonzalo's wife's grandfather, together with other Indians, disinterred Atahualpa's remains and transported them to Cerro Lorango, the highest mountain peak near Cajamarca.

The ashes of the great King of the Incas were scattered in the wind. The Incas believed the condor bird to be a sacred guardian and that Atahualpa's spirit lived on in the form of a condor soaring over the Andes, forever looking down, seeking revenge on his nation's enemies.

...23

THE FIRST DAY of the eleventh month of November. Our trip northwest has been an uneventful 20 days and nights. At noon a sun sight was taken. It placed our vessel at three degrees south latitude. Captain Navarro considered he had gained enough sea room to safely pass Punta Santa Elena (latitude 2 degrees 11' South). He changed course toward Isla de Plata in order to take advantage of the current and favorable wind.

That night off to port, the horizon was becoming obscured and muddled. A few intermittent stars glimmered on the starboard beam. Everyone was aware the galleon was heavily laden. Accordingly, it rode low in the water.

By midnight the wind increased in velocity, coming from the northeast. The seas rose greater than before. It soon happened that we were at the mercy of the wind and water, always being driven closer to shore. I experienced a nagging feeling of uneasiness. Peering over the dark, uncertain horizon, I heard shouts: "Breakers ahead!"

The captain vainly attempted to have the vessel turned into the wind. Taking soundings, he found our ship in five and one-half fathoms and hastily dropped anchor.

A short time later I felt a severe jolt. Captain Navarro later explained that when he saw the breakers, he ordered all sails and anchors dropped. However, he had difficulty getting the anchors down because of mountains of unregistered goods stored on the foredeck and on top of the anchor cables.

After having dinner and taking some stomach medicine, I fell asleep. As I learned later, the severe jolt was caused when the ship's rudder bumped against the reef with such force that it was turned loose from its gudgeon and fell into the sea. As a result, our ship went aground in 4 fathoms of water. The windage from the sails and rigging caused the ship to be dragged over the bottom. Two anchors were dropped. The hooks took hold in four fathoms.

As though in answer to our prayers, in the morning the weather cooperated. By midday the sun was out and the seas calm. Everything was considerably more settled than the previous night. Our hull was sound. A small group of carpenters and crew constructed and installed a new rudder. Assorted pieces of wood and nails were taken from other parts of the ship. Finally, our foresail was raised. The tide flooded by noon. With long poles pushing, the deep-drafted and heavily laden galleon finally floated free. We passed through five fathoms, then six. We were soon in ten fathoms of water, and we watched the bottom disappear from sight. As soon as the vessel safely cleared the shoal, the ship continued its northward journey.

That evening I celebrated the Holy Sacrament, giving thanks for the mercy that had been bestowed upon the ship's company. I recited Psalm 93:4: "The Lord on high is mightier than the noise of many Waters, yea than the mighty Waves of the sea."

THE FOLLOWING MORNING I was informed that Jose Sebastian Barreda, one of my soldier-guards, had suffered a serious head injury, a *commotio cerebri*, or shaking of the brain, during the jolt precipitated by the loss of our rudder. Jose lay in his berth, groaning. I attempted to cheer him up by relating the story of Saint Paul's miraculous survival of a shipwreck.

At first the man seemed not to recognize me. He was delirious. Then Barreda clutched my arm and bluntly asked for absolution. He seemed fearful of going to Hell.

Before absolving the dying man of his sins and administering the last rites, I asked my soldier-guard whether he had anything on his conscience. On his deathbed, Jose Sebastian Barreda confessed being responsible for the deaths of the Indian artisans who had fashioned the gold into Mary and her Holy Child in 1654.

I was appalled to learn His Majesty King Philip IV had issued "secret orders" declaring that none should hear of the Golden Madonna lest rumors would spread, attracting thieves, pirates, or the accursed English.

The king further directed that the skilled Incas who had cast the gold statue should be put to death. Conquistador Jose Sebastian Barreda was sworn to silence after carrying out the king's instructions.

Moments before he died, Barreda muttered, "May God forgive."

Next morning a Mass was held as a memorial for Jose Sebastian Barreda and for a seaman who had fallen from the rigging and drowned when the ship grounded. I thought of my soldier-guard, Jose Sebastian Barreda, and the shocking crime he had committed in the King's name. Only God can forgive. And only God knows the truth of these claims. I'm content to leave it with Him, as I'm a sinner too.

24

THE TENTH DAY of the eleventh month of November. Our ship arrived in Panama at the peak of the heavy rains. The dust had turned to mud, splattering our shoes, socks, and legs. Disease-carrying insects were in abundance. Our clothes were clinging to our flesh, stained with the bloody remains of mosquitoes.

Panama City had a poor harbor and a terrible climate. But it was located on the Pacific side of the isthmus. There were roads across the isthmus via the Las Cruces Trail to Porto Bello. The king's treasure, including my 1800 pound golden statue, would travel on a heavily guarded mule train. The schedule for the trek was closely guarded to confuse would-be ambushers.

The narrow strip of land, the isthmus, was about 40 miles wide at its narrowest point, making it an important link between the Pacific and Atlantic Oceans. All of Europe knew this. And all of Europe wanted to control it, but control of the isthmus fell into the hands of the Spanish. Unfortunately, the rest of Europe periodically raided what they couldn't control.

We were all made aware of the danger from thieves and pirates. Years earlier, Sir Francis Drake had launched a series of audacious raids on mule trains laden with gold destined for the Spanish treasury.

THE TWELFTH DAY of the eleventh month of November. The trip across the Isthmus of Panama over the Las Cruces trail was uncomfortable, unhealthy and dangerous. The road was muddy and slow. The intense heat, the encroaching jungle, and the prevalence of tropical fevers made it a difficult place for foreigners like myself.

I occasionally slept outside my mosquito net because it was too hot. This proved to be a costly miscalculation. After being bitten by mosquitoes, I gathered seeds of the cinchona tree. It was used by the Quechua Indians of Peru to reduce the shaking effects caused by severe chills and fever. I'd been feeling a bit ill for a few days, but I just put it down to an upset stomach and feeling tired.

One evening, I had a stabbing pain in my side, found it really hard to breathe, and felt nauseous. I took a mixture of water and powder that I ground from the cinchona seed and didn't tell anyone about it. I can be very stubborn. I carried on traveling for the next four days until we reached Porto Bello.

After ensuring my cargo was safeguarded in the Church of St. Philip, I sought refuge with the parish priests until my ship was due to sail to Havana. A physician was summoned.

He gave me a bag of cinchona seeds in case I relapsed.

THE SEVENTEENTH DAY of the twelfth month of December. At the time of the cannon signal for weighing anchor, our precious cargo was stored safely on board the frigate *Galera de España.* Prior to our departure to Havana, the Council of the Indies notified captain Don Mendo de Contreras that Oliver Cromwell, the Lord Protector of England, had dispatched a large fleet of ships on a voyage to the West Indies. Although England was officially at peace with Spain, the members of the *Consejo* considered such a fleet could cause Spain serious harm, either by attacking or capturing one or more of our Spanish colonies or by making an attempt on returning treasure galleons.

Double lookouts were posted; however, the days were long and languorous and uneventful, except I was put up in my cabin. Painful stomach cramps and fever prevented me from sleeping peacefully. I lay perspiring on my cot, considering what strange and alien biological germs might be breeding in my intestines. This, with the incessant rolling of the ship, combined to make me miserable.

By the end of December we approached the southern Cuban coastline, giving a wide berth to the rocks of the *Jardines de la Reina.* As the captain cautiously probed his way toward the western tip of Cuba, our lookouts spotted tall English ships on the horizon.

Captain Contreras experienced consternation. Should he stay and fight? Or should he reverse course for a few days in order to protect the king's treasure on board? I prevailed upon the captain to forsake his pride and continue with his mission. Reluctantly the brave commander heeded and my plea prevailed.

We arrived safely in Havana on January 5, 1656. Unfortunately, the Tierra Firme Fleet had already departed for Spain, including the *Nuestra Señora de las Maravillas*, designated carrier for the Golden Madonna. Archbishop Manuel Francisco del Corazon told me the sacred icon would be stored safely in the cathedral in Havana until the next convoy to Seville.

25

THE TENTH DAY of the first month of January 1656. All of Havana is in mourning. We received news of the sinking of the Nuestra Señora de las Maravillas, loaded with more than five million pesos of treasure registered on manifest and much more in contraband.

Archbishop Manuel de Francisco Corazon informed us that four days out of Havana, along the Gulf Stream, the fleet's chief navigator advised the commander they had cleared the treacherous sand shoals of the Bahamas. The order had been given for the fleet to begin its turn to the east when a jagged coral reef appeared on the horizon. A cannon was fired to warn the fleet to alter course. Not all vessels responded to the warning. As the 650-ton Nuestra Senora de Las Maravillas made to come about, she was accidentally rammed by one of the smaller ships.

The crew worked to free the rigging, but water flooded the ship. She settled in 5 fathoms. As plans were being prepared to recover the treasure, a storm moved in. In the ensuing chaos many of the 650 people on board died and the wreckage scattered. Within hours the Maravillas disappeared into the sea and another king's treasure was lost.

My illness has worsened. I find myself staggering around in senseless condition, trying *to come to grips with the situation. A frightful blackness and despair engulfs me. I spend days drifting in and out of consciousness with a high fever, unable to walk or move. I fear my journaling is at an end.*

While I have failed my mission for my Church and my king, let me remind you, I have faithfully sought to be a virtuous priest. Therefore, I ask, please do not judge me too harshly. Perhaps this was God's will or some dreadful curse—I will never know.

In the bleak half-light of dawn, Fernandez read an accompanying note from Carlos Delgado.

Our good padre's written journal is the only record of the 1655 journey of the Golden Madonna from Lima to Havana. Only portions of Badrena's diary were ever recovered. This translated text was stored in the Archivo General de Indias, Seville, Spain. Father Don Emmanuel de Badrena died of malaria shortly after his arrival in Cuba.

PART IV

ATAHUALPA

...26

THE SKY WAS GUNPOWDER GRAY. It had rained during the night. A thick cloud of fog replaced the rain. It was light outside, but overcast. The daylight in the kitchen was gray. Frank Fernandez turned on the lights. His chest ached. He knew he should see a doctor. He went into the bathroom to urinate. He looked in the mirror. He needed a haircut and he needed to lose weight; too much carryout food, pizza and pastries.

Arriving at his office, Fernandez made certain he had copies of Lawrence's backpack contents. He locked the duplicates in his office safe. On an easel he listed the timeline of events.

Sept. 2013: Spain won Odyssey legal case
Oct. 12: Lawrence made offer to Spain
Dec. 15: Spain rejected offer
Jan. 7, 2014: Lawrence requested Maravillas info
March: Spain sent Priest's journal.
April Newspaper: Halsey found gold artifacts
May: Lawrence shifts interest to 1715 fleet
June 5: Lawrence in Ft. Pierce—meets Halsey
          White
July 28: Lawrence contracts with Lazarus Corp.
July 30: Campbell Lawrence murdered
Aug. 2: Halsey White murdered

Fernandez felt he had overlooked something in reading the priest's journal. The devil was in the details. He took a legal pad and reopened the journal. He had no doubts that the priest's information was creditable. In 1656 there had existed a life-sized golden religious artifact ordered by the king of Spain.

Father Manuel Badrena had written of a failed mission. The cargo entrusted to his care had arrived in Havana too late to be shipped on the *Maravillas* as part of an armada bound for Spain.

Frank was trying to follow Campbell Lawrence's reasoning. Now that legal hurdles had been removed as a result of the Odyssey ruling, it was expected that Bermuda would allow salvaging of the *Maravillas*.

But three months later he had lost interest in the *Maravillas*. Why? Fernandez rechecked the dates on his easel. It was clear that Lawrence had shifted focus after receiving the priest's journal. Father Badrena had plainly confessed he had arrived with his cargo too late. So what? Even if Badrena was ill, the Church could have arranged to have someone else accompany the Golden Madonna on the following Spanish treasure fleet shipment.

Why was Lawrence interested in the 1715 treasure fleet? That sailing had occurred 59 years later.

Vesta opened the door, interrupting his concentration. "I reached Ossie Williams's wife, like you asked. Ossie is working a fishing charter today. He will meet you at the marina around three or four o'clock. If they have a big catch, he'll stay a while and clean fish."

IT WAS ALMOST NOON. Frank Fernandez turned away from the computer screen and listened to the quiet murmur of the summer traffic on Seaway Drive. If the FBI was involved, he would recuse himself—even if he had a choice. But he didn't intend to waste any of the remaining hours he had been allotted.

Fernandez opened Campbell Lawrence's folder labeled MAPS. He leaned back in his chair, hands clasped behind his neck. He remembered the newspaper article had referenced the State of Florida sharing ownership in salvaged treasure. Back at the computer, his search led to the Bureau of Archeological Research in Tallahassee.

Tallahassee was a five-hour drive, and there were no direct flights from Melbourne airport. He didn't have time to go to Tallahassee. Another site looked promising: Florida Atlantic University on Glades Road in Boca Raton had a department of anthropology. Dr. Carlisle Mohan was listed as chairman.

Fernandez tapped in the numbers.

A harried voice answered, "Dr. Mohan's office."

"I'm Detective Fernandez with the Fort Pierce Police Department," he said. "I need to speak to Dr. Mohan."

"Mohan here. What's the problem?"

"I'm with the Fort Pierce police," Fernandez repeated.

"Yes. Yes. Lydia told me."

"I need your help, sir. Will you please meet with me?"

After a resigned sigh, he heard, "Of course."

DR. CARLISLE MOHAN WAS A TALL, pleasant-looking man in his mid-forties. He looked like he came from Jamaica or maybe Trinidad. Mohan stood up to greet Fernandez.

"Thank you for seeing me."

"Did I have a choice?" He smiled.

"Two men have been murdered in the Fort Pierce area, a Mr. Halsey White and a Mr. Campbell Lawrence.

Both were treasure salvagers. I am in charge of the investigation."

"Identification, please."

After flashing the gold shield, Fernandez opened his briefcase and withdrew the folder marked MAPS.

"Sir, what can you tell me about these documents?"

Mohan remained standing. He leaned across to examine the papers. "Interesting. They pertain to the Spanish treasure fleet of 1715. We are very familiar with this tragic event." He took a seat. "Coffee?"

"Thank you, black."

Mohan whispered the order into his phone and put on reading glasses. He scanned the papers and then looked up.

"Yes, of course. On July 24, 1715, a Spanish armada of twelve ships sailed from Havana, carrying a cargo of 14 million pesos in gold, silver and jewels. In the Florida Straits the fleet ran into a hurricane. The storm battered the ships; the vessels ran aground and were torn apart. Tons of treasure scattered over the sea bottom. Over 700 people lost their lives. Spanish salvors recovered some of the treasure, but more and more keeps popping up. May I inquire where you obtained these papers?"

"From the backpack of one of the murder victims."

"Ah. I see. Well, let's get started. This is a listing of the ships in the 1715 fleet and a map of the wreck sites."

1 - *Nuestra Señora de la Regla*
Location: Cabin Site south of Sebastian Inlet
27 49.500 N 80 25.400 W
3,500,000 pesos in gold and silver

2 - *Santo Cristo de San Roman*
Location: Corrigan's Wreck-site, south of Wabasso
27 43.800 N 80 22.800 W
2,687,416 pesos of silver and gold

3 - *Nuestra Senora del Carmen San Miguel*
Location: Off Rio Mar Golf Course, Vero Beach
27 38.800 N 80 20.900 W
79,967 pesos in gold bars and doubloons

4 - *Nuestra Señora del Rosario*
Location: Sandy Point Wreck-site south of Vero Beach
27 35.800 N 80 19.650 W
15,514 pesos in gold bars and doubloons

5 - *Urca de Lima*
Location: Wedge Wreck-site North of Ft Pierce Inlet
27 30.326 N 80 17.958 W
Carried 252,171 pesos of privately registered silver

6 - *Nuestra Señora de las Nieves*
Location: Frederick Douglass Beach
27 25.300 N 80 16.500 W
Manifest listed 44,000 pesos in coined silver and bullion

7- Unknown Wreck
Location: Herman's Beach
27 19.000 N 80 12.000 W

8 - *Griffon*
Made it safely back to France

1715 Ships lost and unaccounted for

9 - *Nuestra Señora de La Popa*
Location: La Holandesa Site, Vero Beach
27 43.800 N 80 22.800 W
Carried no treasure

10 - *El Señor San Miguel*
Came apart on reefs in vicinity of Fernandina Beach north
of Jacksonville

11 - *El Cievro*, also known as *La Galleria*
Sunk in deep water—unaccounted for

12 - *Nuestra Señora de la Concepcion*
Came apart off Cape Canaveral

Mohan continued, "As you see, Mr. Fernandez, the
French frigate *Griffon* escaped. Out of the rest, seven have
been found, two are believed to have been found, and
two are somewhere in the Atlantic Ocean—your guess is
as good as anyone's as to where."

After Mohan's secretary came in with coffee,
Fernandez asked, "What would the modern equivalency
of a peso be worth?"

"The 'peso' was a coin known as the 'piece-of-eight' in
English. One piece-of-eight, for example, is valued
somewhere between 100 and 200 dollars. However, the
early Spanish salvagers recovered nearly 80 percent of the
registered treasure on the *Regla* and the *San Roman*, almost
6 million pesos. That still leaves at least 8 million pesos,

worth somewhere between eight and sixteen million dollars.

"The Spanish kept good records, everything meticulously recorded on ships' manifests by scribes working for Spain's House of Trade. The *Casa de Contratacion* governed all commerce to and from the colonies. It was a monopoly. The crown took a Royal Fifth—20 percent of all goods conveyed back to Spain.

"These manifests were preserved, and they reveal an incredible amount of wealth crossing the ocean, and occasionally sinking into it. Remember, for 300 years the Spaniards came over here and stole all of the wealth of the Americas. They would lose about 10 percent of that as the cost of doing business. Several wrecks out there by themselves are worth several billion dollars."

FRANK FERNANDEZ CHECKED HIS WATCH and held up his hands. "I'm on a tight leash. I think the treasure salvagers were murdered because they were on to something connected to the 1715 fleet wrecks."

"I read about Halsey White's death," Mohan said. "I didn't mention it until I knew where this conversation was leading. Halsey White had some wild ideas—"

"The Golden Madonna?"

"Yes. The fabled Madonna of Incan gold: Halsey's Holy Grail. Are you familiar with the Incan empire?"

Fernandez shook his head.

"I urge you to familiarize yourself with the conquest of the Incas. It was King Atahualpa's gold that was used to fashion the statue you are inquiring about."

"What's your professional opinion?"

"I'm not convinced there's anything to the myth. There isn't an archeologist in the world who wouldn't sign away his or her pension to study it. I've talked to other historical experts about the *Maravillas*. They don't believe such a golden statue ever existed.

"If well-financed salvagers with the latest equipment and huge blowers couldn't find a trace of the statue, after years and years of searching the wreck site... well, I can't believe it's really down there in the Bahamas."

Fernandez took out his note pad. "Sir, I have three questions: If there really was a golden effigy ordered by the King of Spain, and if the statue arrived in transit to Havana too late to catch the *Maravillas* in—" He paused to check his dates.

"In the year 1656," said Mohan.

"Right. If the Golden Madonna was shipped aboard the 1715 treasure fleet, how would you explain the long time span?"

"Have you ever heard of the War of Spanish Succession?"

Fernandez shook his head.

"King Philip IV died in 1665, leaving behind one son, Charles, who became Charles II. Charles was both physically and mentally challenged. He was a weak monarch. As a result, the Spanish kingdom suffered decline under his rule. When Charles died in 1700, his will specified that Philip, Duc d'Anjou, grandson of the king of France, succeed him.

"This created a firestorm, threatening the balance of power on the continent. The Holy Roman Emperor Leopold I and other concerned governments opposed. This resulted in the War of Spanish Succession, ending with the signing of the treaties of Utrecht, Rastatt, and Baden, In 1712, Philip V was recognized rightful King of Spain.

"As the war drew to a close, the Spanish Crown was on the verge of bankruptcy. Philip V ordered as much treasure as possible be brought back from the Indies without regard for the cost or dangers involved."

Fernandez said, "Halsey found several pieces that were part of the Queen's Jewels. Is that legend or real?"

"Quite real, I would say. After the death of Queen Maria Luisa of Savoy in 1713, King Philip was married to the Duchess of Parma, Isabel Farnese. Isabel demanded that she be given jewelry 'unique in all-the-world,' or there would be no consummation of the marriage. The king must have been royally smitten, because the duchess's dowry of gold and jewelry was estimated to be worth millions.

"Except for the two items Halsey White dug up, none of the Queen's Jewels have ever been found. In my mind, the old girl's dowry is down there somewhere, covered over by sand, lost to the forces of nature."

"Last question." Fernandez showed Mohan Campbell Lawrence's map. "On which of these ships do you think the Queen's Jewels and perhaps the Golden Madonna were shipped?"

Sebastian
McClarty's
Treasure Museum

✗ Nuestra Senora de la Regla
Cabin Wreck Site
27 49.500N 80 25.400W

Map Of Known —1715— Spanish Shipwreck Sites

Wabasso
Seagrape Beach

✗ Santo Christo de San Roman
Corrigan Wreck Site
27 43.800N 80 22.800W

Rio Mar Drive   **Vero Beach**

✗ Nuestra Senora del Carmen
Rio Mar Wreck
27 38.300N 80 20.900W

Sandy Point Beach

✗ Nuestra Senora De Rosario
Sandy Point Wreck
27 35.800N 80 19.650W

Pepper Beach

✗ Urca de Lima
Wedge Wreck
958W 27 30 336N 80 17

Frederick Douglas Park

Fort Pierce

✗ Nuestra Senora De Les Nieves
Douglas Beach Wreck
27 25.300N 80 16.500W

Jensen Beach

Herman's Beach

✗ Unknown Wreck
27 19.000N 80 12.000W

Mohan smiled. "I'm an academic; you're the detective. However, as an academic I am obliged to quote you Tolstoy. He wrote, 'Truth, like gold, is to be obtained by washing away from it all that is not gold.' Isn't that how investigators go about solving a crime, by eliminating all that is not relevant?"

"Which six ships would you eliminate?"

"*Touche*. The *Nuestra Señora de las Nieves* has always fascinated me. But, after three centuries of everything from ship worms to storm tides, remnants of the *Nieves* could be scattered over ten acres of ocean bottom and covered with sand."

Mohan opened a file. "The little ship was only 192.5 tons and carried a dozen cannons. The manifest registered only 44,000 pesos in gold aboard. Not much. As a result, the Spanish did not seriously salvage the wreck. They were more concerned with the larger galleons. Also, the *Nieves* came completely apart and was scattered along the reefs for more than 3000 feet; the Spanish felt they were wasting their time groping around in murky water for a few handfuls of gold and silver.

"One other thing. The *Nieves* was privately co-owned by its captain and master. It would have been possible to smuggle unregistered cargo in the ship's hull."

Fernandez stood up to go.

"If by chance one of these days you find the fabled 'Golden Madonna,' I'd love to be there when it happens."

"Don't be in such a rush, Dr. Mohan. Two people tried, and they are in the city morgue in Fort Pierce."

ONE HOUR LATER, CHIEF BRUMBERG SAID, "Grab a seat. Did you bring Lawrence's backpack?"

Fernandez nodded. "Lou, don't cut me loose. We're getting close to unraveling both murders."

"It's out of my hands, Frank."

"You want the FBI suits to get the credit?"

Brumberg gave him a long, hard look. "I'm listening."

"Lawrence was a professional treasure hunter. He tried to interest the Spanish government in financing a salvage operation for a Spanish treasure ship that was wrecked in a hurricane off the Bahamas. The Bahamian government banned salvagers, but a recent court ruling opened the door for treasure hunters."

"Where are you going with this, Frank?"

"Spain refused Lawrence's offer. Instead, they sent him declassified, translated documents and a proposal: if Lawrence conducted a successful salvage expedition, and if Spain gained legal ownership of the recovered treasure, they would provide a ten percent finder's fee."

"How generous," Brumberg said.

"The information Spain sent included the journal of a Catholic priest traveling from Lima, Peru to Havana, Cuba in 1656 with a solid gold religious icon he was to shepherd back to Spain. The priest's trip was delayed. By the time they docked in Havana, the *Maravillas* had already set sail.

"Based on my reading of Lawrence's communications with Spain, at this point, he lost interest in the *Maravillas*."

Fernandez felt his adrenaline kick in. "Lawrence spotted the newspaper article about Halsey White recovering a gold chain and ring, which were part of the Spanish queen's dowry. In one of the 'King's Orders' documents it refers to both a golden Madonna and the queen's jewelry to be shipped on one of the 1715 treasure ships. Lawrence thought he could salvage the statue.

"In June, Lawrence contacted Halsey. According to his daughter, Halsey had no money. Maybe he was promised a cut.

"Now Lawrence had to find an investor for the salvage operation and a way to transport the eight-foot gold statue and have it melted into ingots. That's not a do-it-yourself project."

"Doesn't the state of Florida have to be notified?"

"Legally, yes. But Lawrence found an investor who had the means to secretly transport and melt the statue."

He handed Brumberg a copy of the agreement signed by Sheldon Posner and Campbell Lawrence on July 28, 2014.

"This appears to be a letter of understanding between Campbell Lawrence and the Lazarus Corporation. Lazarus agreed to foot the salvaging bill in exchange for half of the current value of recovered treasure.

"Sometime in June, Lawrence was diving off of Fort Pierce. My guess is he was attempting to confirm Halsey's location for the Queen's Jewels and to scout around for his Golden Madonna. Lawrence found it, photographed the statue, and showed it to Sheldon Posner.

"Someone thought Lawrence was getting too close to a multi-million dollar payoff and murdered him. I think the Lazarus people are our number one suspects—just an educated guess."

"It's an interesting story, Frank, but you have no witnesses, no murder weapons, no forensic leads, no tip-offs, no DNA, no fingerprints, greedy heirs. In short, nothing but more of your educated *guessing*."

Brumberg frowned him to silence. "I've got my orders. As of now, your employment with the city is terminated. You can explain your theories to the FBI. They're due tomorrow. Best let me have the badge back when you get a chance."

"Who's the agent-in-charge?"

Brumberg shuffled papers, looking. "Robert Manion."

"Oh shit," Fernandez said. "That's all I need."

...27

AT THE MARINA, THE FISHING BOATS rocked slowly in their moorings. A crowd of people bunched at the railing, watching fish being cleaned. Hungry gray pelicans zoomed closely overhead.

After watching patiently for a few minutes, Fernandez caught the attention of a large, tightly muscled black guy in faded jeans and a strap-style tee shirt.

"Ossie?"

"Give me a few minutes, Boss. I'll be through here."

"Meet me in the Tiki Bar next door."

"No problem. No problem at all."

TEN MINUTES later, Ossie was next to him at the bar.

Fernandez signaled the bartender for a beer. "What are you having, Ossie?"

"Iced tea, thank you, Boss."

"Call me Frank. I'm no slave owner."

Ossie Williams's eyes were solemn, but there was a ghost of a grin on his mouth. "Rich charter folk love to be called Boss. I don't mind; it bulks up the tips."

"I'm investigating the murder of Halsey White. Ellie told me you were a member of his crew in Vietnam."

"That's so."

"What do you know about Halsey White?"

"Captain Halsey was a tough skipper. He saved my ass in Nam and saved it again here."

"Care to tell me about it?"

"After Nam, I couldn't adjust. Nobody appreciated what we had gone through over there. I was in an ugly, downward spiral with drugs and alcohol, in and out of jail. Chief Brumberg was a Vietnam vet. He got Halsey to bail me out twice. My wife, Lisa, was afraid I would hit her. I never did and never would, but I was out of control. She took our boy and went to live in Ocala.

"That last time Halsey bailed me out—I'll never forget it. He barged into my trailer, pulling stuff out of my drawers and closets: empty beer cans, cigarette butts, cocaine in plastic baggies, Valium, and bottles of cough syrup. He said that he didn't save my sorry ass in Nam for nothing.

"I bargained, because that's what addicts do. I promised Halsey I would seek help at any rehab place."

"What did he say?"

Ossie Williams laughed. "The son-of-a-bitch said he was going to rehab me right then and there. Halsey pulled a pistol from his belt. It was loaded. I nearly shit myself. Halsey said he didn't want to witness one of his crew killing himself with drugs and shit. He handed me the gun and said, 'If you have the balls—stop the drinking and drugs and take care of your family. If not, go outside and get it over with, so I can forget what a pantywaist fuck-up my top seaman turned out to be.' "

"Jesus Christ. What did you do?"

"I knew the man saved my life once, and I somehow understood he was trying to do it again. Halsey was challenging my being. It came to that."

Silence.

"I've never had a drink since. Halsey helped me finance my home when the bank wouldn't. He's my son's godfather."

Ossie glowered at Fernandez. "If you find who killed the man, let me know. I'll take care of... things. I owe him that much."

Fernandez reached into his pocket and showed the faded sepia photograph of four men he had taken from Halsey's bedroom. "Recognize any of these people?"

"There's me and Halsey. Next to me is Monk. The other fellow was our gunner's mate, John Lawrence. Johnny never made it back from Nam."

Williams paused before continuing. "In the summer of '68, our patrol river boat was operating in the upper My Tho River. Halsey was boat captain. As we got near the town of Cai Be, a Viet Cong patrol ambushed us with heavy machine gun fire and rockets. In seconds our boat was ablaze, out of control, heading directly for the Viet Cong positions. Johnny Lawrence was wounded in the first Viet Cong barrage, but he kept up return fire from his aft machine gunner's station.

"Halsey was also injured, and his clothes were on fire. He shoved Monk and me into the water toward another PBR. In the face of the fucking enemy fire, Halsey went back for Lawrence, but it was too late; a B-40 rocket exploded, killing Johnny instantly. Halsey saved my life and Monk's too. He got the Navy Cross."

"Who is Monk?"

"That's Mo Carver. He was a member of the UDT, the underwater demolition team assigned to our unit. Mo lives in Okeechobee. We called him Monk after Thelonious Monk, the jazz musician. Mo had the gift for playing piano. I heard they gave him a full music scholarship to a place in New York, but Mo turned it down. His mother was sickly, and his father disappeared when he was a kid."

"The other guy in the picture, John Lawrence. Was Campbell Lawrence John's son?"

"That's true."

"Did you ever meet him?"

Williams hesitated. "No."

Frank sensed that Ossie Williams was holding something back. He let it pass. "I met Halsey White. He told me about the Golden Madonna."

"You mean Halsey's wet dream?"

"You don't think the gold statue exists?"

The big man shrugged. "I think Halsey was lucky to find the queen's stuff he found."

"Do you know where he recovered those items?"

Ossie hesitated before answering. "Probably from one of the 1715 wrecks."

"When Halsey found the gold jewelry, wasn't he required by law to report the longitude and latitude location to the state?"

"Well, you're supposed to list the coordinates of all the blow holes where you find goodies, but Halsey always fudged that information by a couple degrees here and there. He didn't want poachers digging in his holes."

"If you hear of any unusual salvage activities in the area, Ossie, give me a call. Here's my card."

HIS PHONE BUZZED.

"Hi, Frank. Miriam Jolson here. Chief Brumberg notified me that you were off the case. He wants me to meet with the FBI team tomorrow and brief them on autopsy results. I just wanted to say I'm sorry we're not going to be working on this one together. You're thick-headed, but I cringe to think of what Stone Age darlings the Bureau will be sending down."

"Thanks, Miriam. I'm still involved, but not officially. Anything new on the Campbell murder?"

"I was right about the garrote—piano wire."

Fernandez signaled the waitress for a refill.

ON TUESDAY, THE LIBRARY stayed open late.

"Do you have any books about the Incas?"

The young man behind the checkout desk took off his thick glasses and peered at Fernandez. "We close soon, and I'm busy. Look for yourself. It's under the I's in nonfiction."

Fernandez took out his detective badge.

The librarian's complexion paled. He keyed into his computer. "We have one copy on hand of the translated *Cronica de la Conquista del Peru*."

Fernandez walked out of the building with the book under his arm. The librarian yelled, "Wait. I need to see your driver's license. Oh, shit. Never mind."

...28

FOR HOURS FRANK FERNANDEZ read about the Inca Empire; about the invasion by Pizarro's small group of conquistadors, which had led to the destruction of the Inca realm, the plundering of its riches, and the oppression of its people.

Fernandez learned Inca warriors were outfitted in knee-length tunics resembling outfits of Roman soldiers. Their chests and backs were adorned with golden discs called *canipus*. Bright red woolen fringes were worn at the ankles, and on their helmets they wore plumed crests of condor feathers.

He padded barefoot to the fridge and snatched another beer.

In reading further, Frank came upon a passage describing the execution of Atahualpa as "the most evil deed committed in all the empire of the Indies."

The execution took place on 26 July 1563. Atahualpa was taken from his prison to the square. The Inca king was tied to a chair with a thick, scarlet *llautu* rope around his neck, whereupon Atahualpa raised his voice, calling for the faithful to avenge him. He was quickly strangled. In a cruel betrayal, to prevent the Inca king from being mummified, the Spaniards burned his corpse.

FERNANDEZ KNEW HE SHOULDN'T mix pills with alcohol, but he had an annoying headache, and his chest wound troubled him. He took a hydrocodone tablet and went to bed.

He lay in the dark, brooding. His chances of solving the murders lessened with each day that passed. Finally he drifted off to sleep.

A SHORT TIME LATER, Fernandez was awakened by a gentle rapping sound at the front door. He lay motionless for a minute, listening. The rapping continued. He shook off his sleepiness and turned on the light. His eyes looked over at the alarm clock: two-fifteen. "What the hell?" he mumbled.

He went to the door just as he was, in his briefs. Through the peephole he saw a woman standing in the doorway. *How did she get through the security gate?* he wondered. In the pale yellow deck light, her copper skin and dark brown hair framed an exotically beautiful face.

"Wait a minute," he yelled as he grabbed a robe.

Opening the door, Fernandez sniffed an exotic fragrance.

"It is called *White Jasmine*," the woman said. Her smile was warm and friendly and suggested a hint of flirtatiousness. She was dressed casually in black slacks and a cream-colored blouse.

Fernandez wondered who she was and what she wanted in the middle of the night.

"I sincerely apologize for calling at this inconvenient hour," she said. "However, it was a matter of importance."

As if reading his confusion, she shook hands. Her skin was warm. He felt the strong muscle beneath her softness.

"I am Isabel Rojas, from Peru. I need your services."

His first feeling was annoyance. *At 2 o'clock in the morning?* The woman seemed to understand his unspoken protest. She looked at him with a resolute expression that unnerved him. He motioned her to a chair.

"How did you get through the security gate?"

She gave Fernandez a wry smile.

"How did you know the code for the lobby door?"

Isabel Rojas ignored this question also. "I know you are wondering why it was urgent that I contact you, Mr. Fernandez." There was something purifying about the light of her smile when it was cast on him.

"Please call me Frank. Nobody calls me Mr. Fernandez. I am curious. These are not my normal office hours. Is something wrong? What can I do for you?"

"Have you ever heard of Black Lake?"

"Afraid not."

"*Yanacocha* means 'Black Lake,' but the lake is gone, a casualty of parasitic greed. In the city of Yanacocha is the world's most profitable gold mine, run by the Lazarus Corporation."

"I've heard of Lazarus."

"They are corporate conquistadors stealing our gold, like Pizarro and the Spanish."

A shiver ran through him. He wasn't certain if he heard her next response or imagined it.

"Those who steal Incan gold will perish."

She reached across the desk and pressed down gently on his hands. He closed his eyes. He could feel his blood heat up.

"And I know you will help me, Francisco."

"I suppose so," he heard himself echo. "I could try."

Fernandez knew he was dreaming, talking in his sleep. His head was spinning from indecision, from an unbidden lust. He wanted her; it was insane, forbidden. He couldn't remember what happened next.

When he opened his eyes Isabel was on the bed beside him, snuggled up close. Her fingers were gentle, wandering over his body, touching the white scars on his chest. "No hero without a wound," she said. His arms and legs were numb, and he couldn't lift a finger. Her naked breasts and thighs pressed tight against him. She groped his body with her fingers and tongue, raking her nails between his legs.

Isabel straddled him, took hold of his rigid, erect penis and deftly guided it inside her. She took a moment, gathering her breath, and then began slowly rotating her torso.

Her movements grew faster, more pronounced. And before he knew it he was coming inside her. The urge was unstoppable, and like being caught in a rip tide, he surrendered to the current.

...29

IN THE MORNING FRANK FERNANDEZ raised the blinds, and the sun bathed the room in light. He sat on the bed a few moments, wishing he could lie back and sleep. He knew he couldn't; there was a plane to catch. He went to the sink and splashed water on his face. His chest felt tight.

Isabel Rojas came to mind. He hadn't had such a vivid, erotic dream in a long time. The sexual sequences left him feeling guilty. He still couldn't grasp the boundary between the dream and reality.

Fernandez checked the time: 7 a.m. His American Airline flight departed Orlando at 11. On a whim, he booted up his computer and Googled the name she gave him. There were eight pages of listings for Isabel Rojas. One caught his attention.

Isabel Sancho de Rojas ina Atahualpa
Birthdate: 1627, Cajamarca, Peru.
Family: Isabel Sancho de Rojas ina Atahualpa died childless in 1647, the last descendant of Inca King Atahualpa.

140

...30

FRANK FERNANDEZ FASTENED HIS SEATBELT. In preparation for his meeting with Sheldon Posner, he reviewed Campbell Lawrence's LAZARUS file.

Peruvians Halt Gold Mine Expansion

—WASHINGTON POST, July 15th

High in the Andean mountains of Peru is the world's largest gold mine, Yanacocha, run by the Lazarus Corporation of Stamford, Connecticut. In the language of the local Indians, *Yanacocha* means "black lake," but the lake is long gone, a casualty of the mining operation, which extends across fifty square miles.

Mine officials are anxious to expand operations into a nearby mountain called Cerro Quilish, which Lazarus estimates contains more than a billion dollars' worth of gold. For Peruvians, Cerra Quilish is a sacred mountain.

Recently, thousands of Cajamarcans protested the expansion. Local citizens blockaded mining roads and forced the company to cancel its Quilish expansion plans, causing Lazarus stock to dip 25 percent from a year high of $19.12 per share. Lazarus Corporation's CEO, Sheldon Posner, sounded a positive note that the company was actively investigating other lucrative activities.

Fernandez punched in NYSE information on his iPhone. The Lazarus stock had opened at 19.20. The high was 20.12, the low 19.09. *Still way off.* His eyes were tired, and he felt a steel band around his chest wounds. One item in the *Washington Post* article reminded him of something, but the thought vanished. He tilted the seat back and tried to close his eyes.

THE DRIVE TO STAMFORD took over an hour. Fernandez had waited for his rental car and then had difficulty navigating onto the Van Wyck Expressway towards Hutchinson River Parkway and finally I-95 North. He was running late. The dashboard clock read 3:20 when he pulled into the parking area of the Lazarus Corporation headquarters on Gatehouse Road.

His cell phone pinged.

"Mr. Fernandez, this is Ossie."

"What's up, Ossie? I'm late for an appointment."

"You told me keep my ears open. Word on the street is a salvage captain is signing on seamen for a voyage."

What's name of the salvage vessel?"

"*Calusa.* She's docked at Taylor Creek."

"Any idea when they plan to get started?"

"Soon as they get the green light."

"Are you signing on?"

"Me? No. I'm too old."

"I know what you mean, Ossie."

"CAN I HELP YOU?" asked the receptionist.

"I have an appointment with Mr. Posner."

Fernandez noticed the bracelet of gray-colored clamshells, similar to the bracelet worn by Donna Ingram at the marina.

"I don't know whether you've heard, ma'am. Mr. Lawrence was murdered in Florida a short time ago."

"Yes. I know." Her ash-gray eyes clouded over behind the steel-rimmed glasses. She escorted Fernandez down a long corridor. Outside the conference room door she whispered, "Be careful how you deal with these people."

"Come in," Sheldon Posner said.

Fernandez's gold detective's police badge was scrutinized as if it were something he'd bought in a practical-joke store. He managed a brief handshake and glanced around the conference room. There were two people present. Posner had bushy white eyebrows that matched his full head of shaggy white hair.

The Lazarus boss turned to a woman in her late forties. She was dressed in a well-cut, conservative dark-colored suit. Her hair was pulled back and braided. "Meet my lawyer, Meryl Rothstein."

"I'm not sure why we're—"

"Meryl, dear," Posner interrupted. His face took on a resigned expression. "Mr. Fernandez has traveled all the way from Florida. He's investigating a murder."

There was a brisk rap on the door. A man entered. There was something fixed and malevolent about his smile. He was Latino, with a full head of black hair feathered with gray. The man had shifting coal-black eyes. He moved easily, athletically.

"I want to introduce Ray Santiago, our security consultant."

Posner took his little rimless glasses off and began to polish them on his tie. "Now that we are all here, how can we be of assistance in your investigation?"

"As I mentioned on the phone, Mr. Lawrence was murdered on July 30th, and his acquaintance, Halsey White, was murdered three days later."

"Oh my God," Rothstein said through tight lips.

Without waiting for comments from Posner or Santiago, Fernandez opened his briefcase. "Here's what we have so far. Campbell Lawrence was a professional treasure salvager. Starting in December 2013, Lawrence communicated with the government of Spain. He agreed to inform them of any treasure discovered, for which he would get a percentage."

Posner and Santiago exchanged furtive glances.

"Campbell Lawrence planned to salvage a solid gold effigy from one of the treasure ships sunk in 1715. I might add that the icon, an eight-foot Golden Madonna, was rumored to weigh about 1,800 pounds. At today's gold price of $1,188.36 times 26,100 troy ounces, that would be worth about $31 million."

Santiago's eyes narrowed to thin slits.

"The problem was that Lawrence had no money to finance his own salvage operation. That's where you Lazarus folk come in. You signed an agreement with Campbell Lawrence on July 28th. The Lazarus Corporation had the capability to transport an eighteen-hundred-pound object and to melt it down. No muss, no fuss, and no reporting to the state."

Posner's voice dripped with sarcasm. "Let me disabuse you of a few misconceptions. I was sorry to learn of Mr. Lawrence's untimely death. At the time we were interested in investing in his project. Subsequently, my researchers advised me that treasure hunting is a risky investment. Of the six largest salvage projects, all but Mel Fisher's *Atocha* lost money. The news media touts billion-dollar figures when a new wreck is found, but the shares of most public treasure-hunting companies trade at pennies."

Posner's voice was deep and gravelly. "We decided not to pursue the Lawrence project. Further, I resent your insinuation that Lazarus would be a party to any—"

"Let's save time, so I can get back to Fort Pierce at a reasonable hour. Mr. Posner, where were you at 7 am on July 30th?"

The man's low chuckle irritated Fernandez.

"I was at the New York Sports Club on Commerce Road. And on the treadmill next to me was Judge Joseph Pines of the New York State Court of Appeals. Would you like his number?"

"Want to check me out too, bro?" Santiago said with his perpetual smirk. "Bridgeport Shooting Range, every Thursday morning. I shoot with the local cops."

"Mr. Fernandez," Meryl Rothstein said. "I believe your trip was well-intentioned, but futile. My clients have answered your questions. You have a plane to catch."

Posner added, "Your logic is skewed. Presuming we had continued interest, why would we kill the goose who lays the golden egg before we had the egg? Lawrence knew the GPS location; we did not."

Fernandez could feel himself rev up. "Are you certain that with your stock off 25 percent, you weren't interested in a 31 million dollar windfall?"

He watched Posner's face turn a dark shade of crimson and the skin go tight around his jaw.

Meryl Rothstein said, "Mr. Fernandez, you were invited as a courtesy. Now you are abusing our hospitality. Your accusations are libelous."

Sheldon Posner said, "Fortune rarely smiles on the clueless, Mr. Fernandez. If I hear anything more from you, Ms. Rothstein's firm will ensure you use up your paltry pension in legal fees. Please see yourself out."

Fernandez tamped down his building anger. "I'm sure you won't object to my alerting the state of Florida to keep an eye on a vessel, the *Calusa,* preparing to salvage the coastline between Sebastian and Fort Pierce."

He caught them exchanging glances.

Posner looked at Santiago and nodded.

31

IT WAS NEAR MIDNIGHT. Fernandez headed south on the Florida Turnpike. Tiredness was in his bones. He realized the trip had been a waste of time. Posner was spot-on; Lazarus had no motive for killing Lawrence before he led them to the jackpot.

At the Fort Drum Service Plaza, he parked to use the restroom, grab a snack, and order black coffee.

Behind the wheel again, Fernandez considered his options. So far, the case was a failure, with no suspects and no leads in sight. Fort Pierce was small town. Word would get out that he had been canned. His reputation as an investigator would be tarnished. As a result, future business prospects were not encouraging. Fernandez was drawing down his IRA to pay Vesta's salary. There was no good reason to remain in town. His relationship with Maris was over, and he didn't intend to be a ghost father to a ghost son who was not his.

His phone buzzed. He ignored the call.

He took a big gulp of cold coffee and thought about the FBI. Charlie Manion's son would be agent-in charge. Fernandez had done the unforgivable. He had slept with a fellow FBI agent's wife. It had been an unanticipated mistake, but it happened just the same.

In 2008, after the savings and loan scandals, massive mortgage fraud was being exposed. The FBI, because of crippling personnel limitations, was able to assign only 120 agents to investigate and uncover the crimes committed. Those few agents worked around the clock.

Fernandez's wife Arlene couldn't accept his constant travel and late hours. She found someone else.

After the breakup, Frank was morose, depressed, drank too much, and was on the cusp of scuttling his career. At that time, Charlie Manion was on the West Coast, conducting an FBI training session in explosives. His wife, Clara, had been Arlene's best friend.

Clara was concerned about Fernandez's drinking and one night invited him over for dinner. They were both lonesome. One thing led to another. It didn't last long. The Manions patched things up, but Charlie never got the bitterness out of his system.

After a heavy bout of drinking two years ago, Charlie Manion had hatched a plan to kill Fernandez and deposit his body in a Fort Pierce high crime area. Had it not been for one of Vesta's choir boys alerting her, the plan might have succeeded. Manion had died in a firefight with drug dealers on Avenue D. The FBI hushed it up to avert negative publicity, and the police records were sealed.

Fernandez had no idea how much Manion's son knew of his involvement with Clara Manion or his father's death, but he had an oppressive feeling of foreboding.

HIS PHONE BUZZED. It was Brumberg.

"What's wrong, Lou?"

The police chief's voice sounded hoarse. "Terrible news."

Fernandez braced himself.

"I got word. Ellie St. Clair suffered a massive heart attack—she didn't make it."

A jolt slammed through Fernandez as he disconnected the call. He had trouble breathing. He inhaled, taking in big gulps of air. Black specks appeared before his eyes, and he pulled off to the side of the road.

Frank moaned into the silence.

32

OLD, DARK MEMORIES began to stir, images that time and forgetfulness would never erase. Fernandez dreamt he heard the gunfire from the Miami warehouse and the rush of fire into his chest. But this time he was not alone; he was with Ellie. They huddled together in the fading twilight of his consciousness. She didn't speak. Her body was limp. He visualized their last moments together.

"You *will* come to Carmel?"

"I promise," He had told her. "I really promise."

THE FIRST LIGHT OF DAWN outlined the tall palm tree outside Fernandez's bedroom window.

A phone call awakened him.

"This is Ossie Williams. That salvage boat we talked about? Well, it just got the green light for Friday sunup."

"HERE'S WHAT I KNOW," Brumberg said. "The Carmel police told me Ellie St. Clair suffered from a serious heart condition. Her doctors had warned her not to fly across country for Halsey's funeral because the long trip could place too much stress on her heart. I know you two had something going. I'm sorry."

Frank Fernandez and Lou Brumberg looked at each other in silence. The conversation was stalled.

Finally, Brumberg said, "I knew Ellie when she was growing up around here. I don't think I've ever met anyone who seemed more vital and glad to be alive." He shrugged. "But when it comes right down to it, haven't we all had some sort of tragedy happen in our lives that we had problems dealing with? Maybe Halsey's murder was more than Ellie could bear."

Fernandez shrugged. He dropped the gold detective shield on the chief's desk and left without another word.

THE PHONE RANG in his office.

The voice said, "Do you know who this is?"

"Yes."

"I'm in Sarasota, standing in front of 400 Golden Gate Point. Just saw your wife and kid. Nice ass."

Fernandez took in a deep breath. "I hear you."

"Here's the deal: nothing personal. We each have *things* we want to protect. You want the woman and kid to stay healthy; we want you to keep your mouth shut about our little salvage operation. If you talk, I swear on my mother's grave I'll find your family, kill the kid, have fun with the lady, and email you pictures. Are we cool?"

"Yeah."

HE HUNG UP AND PUNCHED IN Maris's number.

"You okay?"

"Why, Frank, I didn't know you still cared."

"Seriously, Maris. Are you and the boy doing well?"

"The boy has a name. It's Charles."

Fernandez was silent.

"We're fine, Frank. Harbor House South is a friendly building. Today I met a nice man on the elevator."

He felt a chill up his back. "What did he look like?"

"Don't tell me you're jealous, Frank. By the way, my lawyer is mailing the divorce papers this week."

Now she sounded like herself again. He held the iPhone to his ear and heard the click and empty silence. It had been a long time since they had really talked.

"DO ME A FAVOR," he said, handing Vesta a slip of paper. "It's important. Use your old contacts and check out a guy name Raymond Santiago."

Vesta Jones was back within minutes. "I Googled the man." She handed him a printout.

In 2004, Raymond Santiago worked in Iraq for a private contractor, Flintlock USA. Santiago, along with other Flintlock employees, was accused of inflicting severe physical and psychological abuse on Iraqi prisoners in Abu Ghraib prison in Baghdad.

Military investigators interviewed dozens of Abu Ghraib prisoners. Their report named Santiago as ringleader of the abuse. One of the prisoners said that one day Santiago struck him repeatedly on the arm with a truncheon, causing multiple bone fractures.

A federal judge dismissed the case, ruling the alleged abuse took place overseas and the U.S. District Court in Alexandria, Virginia, had no jurisdiction.

...33

"THE SUITS ARE HERE," Vesta said.

He handed her a note. "Take care of this. ASAP."

One man stood in the doorway in a white shirt and tie. He was a darkly handsome, serious-looking FBI agent.

"Mr. Fernandez, my name is Manion." He flipped his wallet, displaying his badge. "This is Special Agent Kinkaid."

Kinkaid was tall and lean, in his late forties, with receding gray hair and a strong chin. Kinkaid's gun was in a shoulder holster under his right arm—a bad sign. FBI agents rarely used their weapons. Whenever Fernandez saw someone with a shoulder harness instead of a belt clip, he knew he was dealing with a cowboy.

Fernandez motioned Manion to have a seat; he didn't care if Kinkaid had to stand.

Manion stared at Fernandez for a few seconds, his brow furrowed. "Fort Pierce has sad connotations. As you know, my father was gunned down here."

Fernandez studied the young agent's eyes, searching for anger or sarcasm. It was impossible to tell.

"My mother asked me to say hello. She knew you and your wife in Washington."

Fernandez breathed easier.

Manion took a digital recorder out of his pocket and placed it on the desk. "You've been working the case for a week. We would like to be brought up to speed; you understand?"

Fernandez knew the drill. Manion was going to act friendly and take a baseline reading—see how Fernandez answered things the agent knew to be true. Once he got the baseline, Manion or Kinkaid would ask questions testing Fernandez's stress reactions; then if they sensed he was lying, the session would become an interrogation.

"Coffee?" Fernandez asked.

"No thanks. Do you mind if I take a DNA sample?"

Fernandez understood where he was going with it. Fingerprints and DNA were routinely taken from all persons present at a crime scene; he had been to Halsey's house.

"THE TIME IS 11:30 A.M. August 6," intoned Manion. "Agents Daryl Kinkaid and Robert Manion are interviewing Mr. Frank Fernandez pertaining to the deaths of Campbell Lawrence on July 30th and Halsey White on August 2nd.

"Mr. Fernandez, our investigation revealed the following information, which we would like you to confirm. Okay?"

"Fire away."

"On the afternoon of July 31st, you visited the now-deceased Mr. White. Correct?"

"Correct."

"In fact, you were the last person to see him alive."

"Except for his killer."

"And earlier in the day, Mr. Fernandez, you visited Mrs. Donna Ingram at the Fort Pierce Marina. Correct?"

Fernandez nodded.

"Could you give your answer out loud, please?"

"Yes. I interviewed Donna Ingram."

"What was the purpose of your visit to Mrs. Ingram?"

"Chief Brumberg hired me to investigate the murder of Campbell Lawrence. Sadly, we did not have any leads that panned out. I visited Mrs. Ingram because Lawrence rented a boat slip at the marina. I was—"

Manion interrupted. "You told Chief Brumberg her husband was your prime suspect for Campbell's murder."

"I was wrong."

"In fact," Manion added, "Mrs. Ingram's husband is a Navy SEAL currently in a hospital in Germany recovering from injuries sustained in combat in the Middle East."

"Yes."

The agent flipped some papers. "A few days later you changed your mind and told Chief Louis Brumberg you were certain a large corporation listed on the New York Stock Exchange was responsible for the murders of White and Lawrence. Correct?"

"I didn't say I was *certain*."

"Do you still believe the Lazarus Corporation is involved?"

"No."

"Isn't it also true that your business is floundering? You're in arrears in rent and you have been drawing down your IRA to meet your payroll?"

Kinkaid took over the questioning. "Let me lay it out for you, Fernandez. You wouldn't be the first ex-FBI agent to go rogue. According to BankAmerica, your account is overdrawn. Your business is on the rocks. Your wife is suing for divorce, which will mean alimony and child support payments. You need money."

"That's no crime."

"No, but murder is." Kinkaid's face tightened. "Isn't it true you had a fight in a Hutchinson Island bar with the deceased Campbell Lawrence?"

Fernandez ignored the mockery in Kinkaid's voice, allowing a wave of annoyance to pass, cautioning himself not to be drawn into a confrontation at the outset of this interview.

"Is it correct that you were on the swim team in college; made the finals in 500 yard freestyle championships?"

"Correct."

"Did you find out where Campbell Lawrence was salvaging for gold, swim out and strangle him?"

"Nonsense."

"According to your phone records, you arranged to meet Carlisle Mohan, director of the Department of Anthropology of Atlantic University. Dr. Mohan reported that you presented your badge and questioned him about sunken treasure, particularly a golden religious relic. You inquired as to which ship it would have been on and how much it would bring on the open market."

Fernandez thought, *Bank records, phone records. These clowns are serious.*

Vesta came in and handed him a note.

Kinkaid continued. "We contacted Donna Ingram in Germany. She claimed you harassed her. You are a piece of work, Fernandez. You even slept with Halsey White's daughter to—"

Fernandez checked his watch. He leaned towards the microphone. "Interview with Mr. Fernandez stopped at 11:39 a.m.

"Switch the recorder off," he demanded. "Ellie St. Clair died this week of a heart attack. I won't have you even discussing her." The mood in the room grew oppressive. No one could miss the tension between the two men.

"You are a piece of work," Kinkaid said. "Don't tell me—"

Fernandez rose, feeling some of the age that stiffened his joints. He took a few steps until he was inches from Kinkaid's nose, forcing the agent to stagger backwards.

He glared hard at Kinkaid and pointed three stiffened fingers at the man's windpipe.

"I'm out of shape, but it will take two seconds to keep you quiet for a month."

Kinkaid's face flinched and paled. He raised his hands, palms out, and flashed a forced smile. "Just doing my job, Frank. Sorry. Nothing personal."

"Okay, kiddies, fun's over. At sunup on Thursday, July 30th, and again Sunday, August 2nd, I was swimming laps at the main pool in Ocean Village. Here are the names and phone numbers of eyewitnesses: the pool man, Karl, and the building cleaning crew—all six in total. Their boss is named Sarah. Call her. Now, both of you, get the fuck out of my office and out of my life."

As Robert Manion left, he flipped Fernandez the bird.

Vesta said, "That agent is the spitting image of you."

"Don't be ridiculous."

"How well did you know the boy's mother?"

Fernandez felt his face redden.

"Do the math, honey. Do the math."

OSSIE WILLIAMS was in Frank Fernandez's office drinking iced tea. "From what I heard, Captain Collins wants his crew on board by 5 a.m. for a 'first-light' departure. At that hour things are quiet, fewer people nosin' around. Skip Collins doesn't have a good reputation."

"How do they know where to salvage?"

"If Collins has the old man's log, he'll use a GPS to plot the latitude and longitude of Halsey's hole. But you don't just hop on a salvage boat loaded with electronic gadgets and head for gin-clear waters. Most times the water is so murky you don't find anything on the first dive, and sometimes not on the tenth. Storm tides and strong currents move stuff around. Even with state-of-the-art detecting gear, you're never guaranteed of nothing."

"Assuming Collins salvaged the gold statue, it's got to be melted down. Where would they go to do that?"

Ossie shook his head.

Fernandez tapped into his computer. "Lazarus has a division in Wilmington, North Carolina: MP Precious Metals Refining, LLC. That's where the gold would be melted down. Once Posner transports the gold statue to the refining company, he's in position to net 30 million dollars."

"Why are you so fired up, Frank? That's the way it is. The rich folk get the gold statue, the rich sugar growers pollute the Indian River, and the governor's rich cronies get a high-speed train roaring through Fort Pierce all day long. The politicians are in the pockets of rich white folks. Get used to it."

Fernandez flipped over a fresh sheet on the easel.

"I need your help finding where the *Calusa* will salvage."

"I should be getting home."

"Please give me a few more minutes."

Williams scowled. "Tell me where they found Lawrence's body."

Fernandez dug out his notebook. "Offshore from Bathtub Beach in Stuart at approximately 9 a.m. Thursday, July 30th. His boat was discovered by the Coast Guard three hours later—drifting south."

"And when did the man die?"

"According to the coroner, 7 a.m."

"Do you know the current and wind speed?"

Fernandez flipped pages, furrowing his brow. "I have it somewhere. Here we go. Coast Guard reported, 'At 0800 July 30, north winds around 10 to 11 knots, increasing to 12 knots in the afternoon. Seas 2 feet with a light chop.'"

"Write this down. We got two hours of drift to the south at 10 to 11 knots. Knots are the same as nautical miles, so mark down 20 to 22 miles. Now multiply by 1.15 to get us regular miles."

Fernandez jotted 23 and 25.3.

Ossie stared at the numbers, musing aloud. "The Gulf Stream current runs north at about 4 miles an hour. So knock off 8 from your numbers. Good. That leaves us with a drift distance from the killing point of about 15 to 17 land miles."

Fernandez whistled silently.

"You got a map of the area?" Ossie asked.

"I can pull it up on the computer and print it out."

"Measure off 15 to 17 miles north of Bathtub Beach."

"The map scale is ½ inch to the mile," Fernandez said. "I'll average the difference to 16 miles. That's 8 inches on the map.

"I'll be damned, Ossie; you are one smart son-of-a-bitch. Campbell Lawrence was murdered off Frederick Douglass Park."

"If it's the *Nieves* wreck they looking for, Frank, don't mess with these guys. Collins' crew will be armed. Some sharks walk on two legs."

PART V

THE *CALUSA*

...35

SANTIAGO WAS CAPABLE OF MURDER. Frank
Fernandez worried about Maris. He couldn't sleep. He
knew if he told anyone about the *Calusa*, he would be
risking his ex-wife's life. Posner's henchman wouldn't
hesitate to kill Maris and the kid. Why should he be
involved? Sheldon Posner had broken no laws.

Fernandez got out of bed. In the bathroom he downed
a hydrocodone tablet. He was in pain and needed to
sleep. His eyes grew heavy and closed.

IN HIS DREAM FRANK WALKED UP a rope-lined
path to where seagrass gave way to fine white sand. All
was silent except for the gentle lapping of the waves. The
ocean was mirror smooth and the beach bare of trees.
Vine-covered dunes dotted the shoreline.

He saw a figure gliding across the beach to the water's
edge. It was Isabel Rojas, wearing a headdress of long,
shiny black feathers. The royal shield on her chest was a
picture of the sun god made of hummingbird feathers.
She wore heavy gold bracelets and earrings. Around her
bare ankles was scarlet-colored knotted rope.

"Isabel," he yelled.

She seemed not to hear him.

Frank tried to move toward her, but his body felt
encased in thick syrup.

Isabel raised her right hand toward the rising sun.

O Great Ruler Atahualpa,
We are no longer the mighty Inca.

The Sun has been challenged
By pagans who care not for our land
Only gold from sacred Cerro Quilish.

Whither now, Atahualpa,
O King of the Inca
As I stand before the Sun
Let the god of storms
Toss his balls of thunder
And cast his reeds of lightning

O Sovereign King Atahualpa,
I invoke thee once again
To help me punish our enemies
To avenge thee my Grandfather
Thank you for hearing my cry

"Isabel, Isabel," Fernandez called out.

The Inca princess turned to face him. She stared with large, black, piercing eyes.

A strange fog descended.

He heard a hissing sound. Isabel was gone.

...36

THE *CALUSA* ROCKED GENTLY, creaking against her ropes at the Taylor Creek Marina. A forest of swaying rigging and halyards clanked against aluminum masts.

In the predawn light, pelicans, akin to prehistoric pterodactyls, folded their wings and dropped like stones into the Indian River.

Skip Collins was a sixty-year-old, six-foot-two, silver-haired, steely-eyed captain. His idea of recreation was riding his Harley or swimming with hammerhead sharks. Collins and Sheldon Posner were alone in the wheelhouse. Posner opened a briefcase and extracted a single sheet.

Collins said, "This is from Halsey White's log."

The captain shrugged. *No skin off my ass*, he thought.

Depart Ft. Pierce Inlet at 08:00 August 12
Arrive Nieves wreck site 08:20
Seas unusually calm with winds SE at 5 kts.
Water clear, with visibility 20' or more.

Sandy flat bottom with depth of sand 6 –
8 feet over limestone –Anastasia rock
09:00: Working sanded-over rocky ridge,
200 yards off Frederick Douglass Beach.
Metal detector buzzed. It was a beer can.
Metal detector buzzed again. Another hit.

Fanned through 6 –8 inches of sand
Found gold necklace and dragonhead ring.

Hole location 27 25.300 N 80 16.500 W

Collins plotted Halsey's GPS reading.

"Approximately 4 miles south of the inlet. Looks like the target object is located directly east of Frederick Douglass Park, 200 feet off the beach in 15 feet of water—between two ridges."

"How long is this job going to take?" Posner asked.

"In salvaging there are no guarantees. Halsey's GPS fixes a position relative to military satellites circling the earth converted to longitude and latitude. It's accurate to within fifteen feet, but salvage pros like Halsey White usually add or subtract a degree or two from the GPS reading they logged in to keep the information secure.

"In addition, you can drop a coin on the beach and the next day it could be buried under two feet of sand. We're hunting for something that has been on the bottom of the ocean for over 300 years. Fifteen feet can—"

Posner interrupted. "Let me make myself perfectly clear, Collins. I'm told you're one of the best salvagers in these parts and you know how to keep your mouth shut. I am paying top dollar for your service. I expect results—not excuses."

Collins looked at the owner's reddening face. He made no attempt to answer the deliberate insult. He decided that it would be wiser to explain to the asshole what standard salvaging steps were to be undertaken. Otherwise, Posner might sue him for non-performance or withhold payment for the job.

"My plan is to put out three anchors at the Frederick Douglass site about dawn. At that time the place is pretty much empty. Amateur salvagers usually operate only on weekends. I would like to get in and out in one day. Otherwise, we try again Monday."

Collins continued. "We'll start by operating the side scan sonar that electronically records acoustic imagery on the sea bottom. The image is like a photograph. We don't want to be wasting time on beer cans and iron scrap. If we get a positive reading, I'll send a two-man team down with hookah rigs, which are air suppliers feeding off a compressor. They will use a magnetometer to search the area where Halsey's Queen's Jewels were found. If we don't strike pay dirt by 10 o'clock, I'll send a couple of guys down with scuba tanks. They can check around the bottom further away from the boats."

Posner wasn't pleased with that prospect.

"If no hits by noon, I'll lower blasters by crane over the stern attached to the transom. With the blasters we can force the propeller wash into the tubes and blast through 20 feet of sand and clear a hole 60 x 35 feet."

"And if that doesn't work?"

"We leave the three anchors in place. I can move the boat in 6-foot increments by shortening and lengthening the front anchor lines. When we find the statue, depending on the time of day, we will grapple it into a cradle and decide when to raise her."

"Why the hell would you wait?"

"Mr. Posner, gold is as shiny after 300 years under water as it was the day it was loaded aboard ship. Frederick Douglass Beach is a popular spot. Everybody and their brothers have digital phones that take great pictures. Unless you want to be on CNN, it is better for us to move off shore a few miles and raise the statue at night.

"I'll put a small buoy over the spot. After dark we use lights, but it shouldn't take long. The crane you had retrofitted has a seven-ton capacity. Do I have your approval to proceed?"

Posner grunted permission.

At 0600 hours, Captain Collins gave the command, "Let go all lines." Mo Carver took the helm. The *Calusa* slipped out of the Taylor Creek Marina into the cool air of a shark gray dawn.

...37

"PROBLEMS, BOSS," Captain Collins said.

"What kind of problems?" Sheldon Posner made no attempt to hide his irritation.

Collins handed Posner the weather advisory.

STORM WARNING: National Weather Service
Tropical Depression accelerating into dangerous storm. Severe weather imminent. Areas affected: Port St. Lucie County, Martin County and adjacent Atlantic coastal waters. At 7 am EDT, the center of storm was located near Latitude 27.25 N, Longitude 80.16 W, approximately 100 miles southeast of Cape Canaveral, FL, one mile east of Fort Pierce, FL. Serious threat of flooding and beach erosion in affected areas. Hazardous boating advisory: Banded rainsqualls could produce dangerous winds of 50 to 75 knots and seas 25 to 35 feet. The next local update will be issued by the National Weather Service in Melbourne at noon EDT, or sooner if conditions warrant. Storm Watch remains in effect.

"Some freaky, early-season storm heading our way," Collins said. "The sky looks dark. The wind is starting to kick up, and I smell heavy rain on the way. We ought to return to port."

"What the hell are you talking about? We're close to shore. Don't be a pussy. You won't melt in the rain."

"It's your nickel, boss, but I've got a bad feeling."

By 7 am, the sun was blotted out by black clouds. The wind gained in velocity. Threatening rumbles of thunder preceded lightning streaks.

On the south and southeastern horizon, the rapidly growing banks of clouds had a strange and ominous quality. The ocean turned from beautiful to ugly in less than thirty minutes. The rushing of the wind grew louder. Slate-colored waves and foaming water splashed halfway up the sides of the *Calusa*.

Seagulls screeched on outspread wings overhead.

The wind rose to 50 miles per hour, and waves climbed to 25 feet. The *Calusa* rolled like a roller coaster, creaking and groaning. The seas became heaving mountains that rushed out of sheets of pouring rain. On the bridge, the half-inch safety glass burst as if a wrecking ball had hit it. Water inundated the wheelhouse, flooding the electrical circuits. The lights went off amidst smoke and wires crackling.

Collins' voice was lost in the howling wind. He used hand motions to direct crewmembers in their unsuccessful attempt to nail canvas and plywood over the windows.

Incredibly, the storm increased in its fury. Collins found himself fighting to keep the ship on a steady course while being whipped and deluged by the driving rain. He didn't know where Posner had gone and didn't care. *I should never have listened to that fat fucker.*

ANOTHER ROGUE WAVE avalanched over the deck, burying the *Calusa* under tons of water and pushing her over on her beam ends. Collins looked out the side windows of the wheelhouse directly into the menacing gray waters. He heard the wind make a sound he had never heard before, a deep tonal vibration—a woman moaning.

Collins called the Coast Guard on his satellite phone. Over the static and wind shriek, he said, "This is the *Calusa*, off Fort Pierce Inlet. We took a hell of a freak wave: cresting maybe thirty feet high. We went way over on our side. I wasn't sure we would make it back up. It took three windows out of the bridge, and we lost all our instrumentation. It's pretty rough."

"Are you in danger, or can you ride out the storm?"

"Well, we're in danger. Definitely in danger. If we get any more water coming through the bridge, that's going to wipe out any communications we have left. We're shored up. Everything is battened down. I'm going to try and get back to port."

The *Calusa* righted herself again, and Collins checked for damages. The batteries had come out of their boxes. The marina was 30 minutes north. He knew the risks. If he stayed on course, the *Calusa* might capsize in the deep troughs. If he turned the ship in the storm, he would have to keep from broaching when the boat was broadside to the breaking waves. Even a minute or two could be long enough to get rolled over. Steel-hulled vessels don't easily recover from broaching; they downflood and sink.

"Bring her around, Mo," he ordered.

"The waves will pound us broadside."

"We'll sink if we don't!" Collins snapped.

Lightning flashed. Thirty-foot waves pounded the ship.

"I'm trying to bring her around," Carver grumbled as lightning flashed and thirty-foot waves pounded the ship. "She's not responding."

Collins nodded in grim silence. He added his strength to that of the helmsman as they struggled to bring her around. Slowly—too slowly, it seemed to Collins—the hull slewed broadside to the onslaught of the seas that smashed into the entire length of the ship. After what seemed an eternity, the *Calusa* righted herself. She had survived the 180-degree turn without broaching.

"Holy shit," muttered Mo Carver. "That was close."

"I'll steer her to the inlet," Collins said. "Check below for damage." Collins was bleeding from the scalp. He could feel it running down his face in warm streams.

A LOUD EXPLOSION rocked the boat.

"What the fuck?" Collins exclaimed. He heard a loud hissing sound as seawater surged through the burning hull. Steam mingled with smoke. The ship was out of control. The explosion had crippled the engines, and there was no steerageway. After that, downflooding occurred. Collins knew the *Calusa* was dead in the water and in danger of sinking.

Smoke continued to pour into the wheelhouse. Collins and Carver were forced off the bridge, choking and coughing from the fumes. Any hope of saving the *Calusa* had evaporated. They found Sheldon Posner clinging to the crane with both arms.

At 8:15 the Coast Guard station at Port Canaveral picked up a voice on VHF: "Mayday. Mayday! This is the salvage ship *Calusa* at the mouth of the Fort Pierce Inlet. We are sinking. If anyone can hear us, pass our position on to the Coast Guard. Repeat, this is a mayday. If anyone can hear us, pass out position on to the Coast Guard. Mayday! Mayday!"

The full force of the storm continued pounding the ship. A dazed Sheldon Posner released his grip from the crane and grabbed Collins' arm, screaming, "Do something."

As if driven by some unearthly force, another wave surged across the ship, sweeping Posner off the deck and over the side.

Collins reacted instinctively, throwing a ring buoy overboard and shouting to his employer. Posner appeared not to hear. The man coughed and gasped violently. The life preserver dropped right in front of him, but Posner made no attempt to grab it. For the rest of his life, Collins would swear some unseen force had dragged Posner underwater. Others would say it was a rip tide.

The tempest seemed to immediately moderate. The rain subsided, but a thick cloud of fog replaced it. He heard the engines finally stop and felt the boat begin to list. Taking advantage of the lull, Collins called out, "Abandon ship! Pass the word. Abandon ship!" Crew members leaped off the upending bow and swam the short distance to Fort Pierce Beach.

After ensuring that no one remained on board, the *Calusa's* captain lowered himself over the side into the water and swam until it was shallow enough to stand. He could see flickering blue lights on shore and hear sirens. Skip Collins looked back as the half-sunken boat drifted away and disappeared into the fog.

...38

A JAGGED SHEET OF LIGHTNING preceded a shuddering bass boom. The wind gusted hard enough to send palm fronds thudding against Frank Fernandez's bedroom windows. He was jarred awake. The red digital numbers on the clock radio read 07:20.

A few faint streaks of light penetrated the dense fog. Heavy rain drummed against the building. By the time Fernandez put the coffee maker on and dressed, the storm had faded to a few faint rumbles somewhere over Lake Okeechobee.

Frank remembered his dream of Isabel standing on a beach wearing a headdress made of black feathers, her hand raised toward the sun. He closed his eyes, trying to replay the dream, but he couldn't get it. On the television he heard a special bulletin.

This is Channel 5 late-breaking news. A sudden squall with record waves and shrieking winds up to 120 mph hit the coastline before daylight at Hutchinson Island near Fort Pierce. All boat traffic has been halted going in and out of the Fort Pierce Inlet after the treasure salvage vessel Calusa *sank early this morning. Vessel owner Sheldon Posner is reported dead, and one crewmember is missing. Portions of the Treasure Coast shoreline, particularly in St. Lucie County, experienced severe erosion. In other news...*

His phone rang.

"It's Vesta. You heard about the ship sinking?"

"Yeah."

"My partner's with the fire department. She told me that the ship blew up."

"What do you mean, blew up?"

"Somebody planted explosives on the *Calusa*."

FRANK FERNANDEZ BREWED COFFEE. He wondered who had had a motive to stop Sheldon Posner from harvesting the gold statue.

He remembered Ellie St. Clair looking at Halsey's photograph and saying, "The big man on the right looks like Ossie Williams. Ossie treasure salvaged with Halsey."

Fernandez searched in his briefcase until he found a copy of the newspaper article. He booted up his computer and checked the number of the local newspaper. He punched it in on his phone and hit 4 for the newsroom.

"Hello. I'm with the Fort Pierce Police Department. Can you tell me the name of the reporter who wrote the article on May 24, 2014, entitled 'Fort Pierce Treasure Salvager Strikes Gold'? ... Yes, I'll hold... The reporter is Alise Smith? Is she in?"

"Smith here."

"Good morning, Ms. Smith. My name is Fernandez. I'm working with the police on an investigation. You did the article on Halsey White that appeared on May 24th."

"Yes, I did."

"In your article you didn't mention whether Captain White was salvaging alone when he found the items you described."

"Why don't you guys get your act together?" Alisa Smith snapped. "You're the second call in an hour asking the same question. Jesus."

Fernandez remained silent.

"I checked my notes. The article was edited and shortened by some idiot upstairs. Captain Halsey White had help. It would have been too dangerous to for an old guy like that to use a hookah line and work alone. His partner's name was Williams."

THREE DAYS EARLIER, Ossie had warned, "Stay out of this, Frank; it don't concern you." He considered the probability and logical assumptions of Ossie Williams's involvement. The man was left-handed and strong as a bull. He had lied about not knowing Lawrence. He had a background of drug abuse.

Ossie Williams was aware there might be a 30-million-dollar jackpot near the spot where he had salvaged the Queen's Jewels with Halsey White. And he knew how to handle explosives from his Viet Nam experience.

Fernandez concluded that this time, Ossie wouldn't let the rich folk win. He sighed heavily. He felt used up and incompetent. He had been scammed.

...39

IN THE LATE AFTERNOON a light misty rain was falling. Chief Lou Brumberg telephoned. "Frank, the Coast Guard and Corps of Engineers claim they have no jurisdiction for investigating the ship sinking. The mayor is sucking up to the press. He wants to show his police force is doing something, that we're not paralyzed. Even though we are. I'm asking for your help... as a friend."

"I need to talk to you, Lou. It's very important."

"Save it for later, Frank."

CAPTAIN SKIP COLLINS WAS SITTING in the chief of police's office, drinking coffee, when Fernandez arrived.

"Sorry about your boat accident," Fernandez said.

"Sure as hell wasn't an accident. And it wasn't my boat. I was hired on as temporary captain."

Brumberg gave Fernandez a nod to proceed.

"How are your crewmembers?"

"My first mate, Mo Carver, received first-degree burns. He'll be okay." Collins shrugged. "My two Hispanic divers had green cards. They're long gone."

"Anybody else on board?"

"Just the owner, Mr. Posner, and his security guard."

"Walk me through the sinking, Captain."

"I'm in between jobs. Mr. Posner hired me—"

Fernandez broke in. "Posner was the man who died?"

"Yeah. The asshole."

"Go ahead."

"Posner hired me to manage a short-run salvage trip and then take the boat up the coast. Sometime after dawn, Mo Carver handed me a weather warning from the National Weather Service. It was serious enough to head back to port.

"Posner blew a fuse. He called me a pussy. He insisted I stay on course. Then all hell broke loose. I've been around a long time. This storm was a freak, with high waves and wind. As a precaution, I called the Coast Guard and advised them I was trying to turn and head north. That's a dangerous maneuver in rough seas. We could have rolled and broached. Mo Carver helped at the helm, and we were able to turn the *Calusa*. One of the big problems was the crane. It made us top-heavy.

"Luckily, we had brought the ship about when the goddamn crane busted loose, knocking Posner head-over-ass into the water. As suddenly as it started, the rain stopped.

"Then I heard two explosions, and black smoke poured out of the engine room. The blasts had ripped the hull open; water poured in, flooding the boat. I ordered everybody to abandon ship. We were about 100 yards off Fort Pierce Beach.

"What happened to Santiago?" Fernandez asked.

Collins shook his head. "No idea. With the ship burning to the waterline, I was lucky to get off myself."

"What are your plans now, Collins?"

"A rich guy from Arizona wants me to head up a salvage expedition off the coast of Ireland, the *RMS Lusitania*. My client's been fighting with the Irish government for permission to salvage. I got an email this week. He's ready to roll."

Fernandez studied Collins' eyes and felt the man was telling the truth, or else he was an accomplished liar.

There was a knock at the door.

"Yes," Brumberg shouted.

His secretary came in and whispered in his ear.

"Oh, shit!" the police chief muttered. "Ossie Williams' wife called. She's hysterical. Ossie's been murdered."

...40

TWO POLICE CARS stood in front of Ossie Williams' house with their blue lights flashing. A waist high chain-link fence and a swingy gate pitted by salt air marked the front yard. A crowd of neighbors gathered under umbrellas in the rain.

"What's going on, Jenkins?" Brumberg asked the officer stationed outside.

The man's voice was thick, his eyes red-rimmed in an unnaturally pale face. "It's enough to make you puke, Captain. The guy was tortured."

"Who's inside?"

"Medical examiner, crime lab, and FBI guys."

"Where's Mrs. Williams?"

"They took her to the emergency room."

AS SOON AS FRANK FERNANDEZ ENTERED, he had to stop for a moment and catch his breath. Ossie Williams lay slumped over the table. He had been shot in the forehead.

There was the smell of vomit. When Fernandez looked at the victim's hand, he saw caked black blood, and something missing. Ossie Williams's index finger had been removed. All that remained were black threads of coagulated blood and a glistening tendon end.

"What the hell are you doing here?" Manion said.

Lou Brumberg cleared his throat. "Frank no longer has the status of a police consultant. He's here solely as a favor to me."

"Well, stay out of our way—old timer."

Fernandez saw the spark of flint in Robert Manion's eyes. He understood him. He had been like that once.

"You're looking peaked, Frank," Miriam Jolson said.

"Fill me in."

"Somebody wanted information. My guess is they got it. The severed surface of the amputation suggests the killer used an industrial blade of some sort to cut through the bone. I'll know more when I do the autopsy."

"Was the killer left-handed or right handed?"

"With the blade, I can't tell."

Fernandez studied the circular hole in Ossie Williams's forehead.

Jolson added, "There is black, congealed blood around where the bullet entered and burn marks on the skin from the shot. That means the shot was fired at close range and at a downward angle."

"Can you tell what kind of weapon was used?"

Jolson shook her head. "The pathologist will figure that out. The burn marks suggest a short-barreled handgun."

"Did you find any DNA or prints?"

"The crime lab boys photographed wet shoeprints of the killer. And I've got a couple of hairs that might belong to anybody."

"Any signs of a break-in?"

"No."

"Probably picked the lock," Manion said.

"People only pick locks on TV."

"Fuck you, Fernandez."

After Manion stalked away, Jolson said, "That young man has your looks."

"Yeah. I've heard that before."

"And your sweet disposition, too."

Fernandez used to instruct his FBI trainees that first impressions were often the most important, while your senses were on high alert, before they were blunted and counteracted by the forensic team's dry facts.

"Don't search for something," he would say. "Just search. If you search for something, your mind is closed to other stimuli."

He knew he was out of practice, but he tried to take in the crime scene. He walked through the connecting door to the garage. A sensor light went on automatically. He divided the garage into squares and scanned the walls the way he had taught recruits.

Fernandez rummaged the empty boxes. One was labeled *CS Unitec Underwater Tools*. He opened the lid. Inside were assembly instructions for an underwater portable hacksaw. The literature specified the saws were ideal for deep-water salvage operations, including cutting pipe, structural steel, and cast iron.

"I've got something."

Jolson gave Fernandez a life-weary expression.

"An underwater power hacksaw."

"For God's sake, why?"

"To cut gold."

"I need to talk to Ossie's wife."

Brumberg shook his head. "The woman is in shock."

"It can't wait. There is a serial killer loose."

...41

IN THE LAWNWOOD EMERGENCY ROOM, Frank Fernandez was led to a curtained-off area. Mrs. Williams had the dark, sad, worldly eyes of a woman beaten by life. Fernandez cleared his throat.

During his years in the FBI, he had interviewed many people who had lost loved ones to violence, but it never got any easier. Fernandez never knew with the victim's relatives how to strike the right balance between professionalism and sympathy.

"We know this is extremely difficult for you, Mrs. Williams. I have to ask you a few questions. Tell me if you don't feel up to it; I can come back tomorrow."

"Best get it over with."

Her dark face was swollen, her eyes red and tearful. Fernandez felt the woman had lived a hard life. He chose a chair opposite her bed, sat down, and gave her a brief smile. "How are you holding up?"

"How do you think?

The woman brought both hands to her mouth, sobbing silently.

He felt embarrassed with his clumsy introduction. "Is there anything I can do for you?"

There was dull sorrow in her voice. "Can you raise the dead?" He could hear the rasp of her breath as she tried to get herself under control.

"I'm terribly sorry for your loss. I have been hired to investigate what happened to Ossie. Was your husband worried about anything recently?"

She wiped her eyes with her sleeve. "No," she answered. "Nothing I can think of."

"Was there anything in your husband's work or private life that might have made him enemies?"

Lisa Williams stifled a sob. "Ossie was a good man, a hard-working man. He had his share of troubles a few years back, but the captain straightened him out. And then he got the cancer."

"What was Ossie's relationship with Halsey White?"

"Halsey was like a father to Ossie."

"Why did your husband order a hacksaw?"

"I'm not supposed to talk about it."

"Why not?"

The woman looked exhausted. "Had to do with salvaging off Colored Beach."

"I understand that your husband served in Viet Nam with a man named Mo Carver?"

"Yes, poor man. Ossie used to say, 'If Mo didn't have bad luck, he wouldn't have no luck at all.'"

"Why would Ossie say that?"

"Mo got into drugs the war. They all did. Ossie too, but Captain Halsey put Ossie to right.

"Mo played piano. When he came home from the war, he traveled with a band. Then the drugs got to him. He was arrested."

Lisa Williams drank some water. "While Mo was in prison, he had a bad accident. After that, Mo never played the piano again. Captain Halsey helped him get parole and set up a music store in Okeechobee. Last year Mo Carver's music business dried up, and he took to treasure salvaging."

Fernandez remained silent.

"Ossie said Mo was riled over his daughter."

"Daughter?"

"Donna. She's married to the Navy SEAL man."

"Why was Mr. Carver upset?"

"That Lawrence fellow made Donna with child."

Fernandez cast his eyes down to his notebook. It was blank. "Thank you, ma'am," he said.

DID FRANK FERNANDEZ miss the FBI? Did he miss profiling sick souls who tortured people with gruesome acts of brutality? No, but he missed the importance of it. He missed the feeling that he was helping. He missed being actively involved. It was as simple as that. He drove to the police station.

Fernandez took the plunge. "We are close to solving this one, Lou. I know who the guilty party is."

"Enlighten me for the fourth time this week."

"My first FBI boss always said 'Find the money. Find the money and follow it. It will always lead you to the answer.' Halsey believed there was a golden statue of the Madonna and the infant Jesus lost in a shipwreck off the Bahamas. It was Halsey's Holy Grail, but one he never expected to find at his age and with his infirmities.

"Along came his dead shipmate's son with evidence that the golden artifact was never on the *Maravillas*; it had arrived too late from Peru. Lawrence had documents proving the statue was shipped on the 1715 treasure fleet.

"Lawrence concluded a golden Madonna was on the same ship as the Queen's Jewels, which was the *Nieves*. Ossie's widow said that when Lawrence came to Fort Pierce, Halsey White was born again. He found his Jesus."

Brumberg drummed on his desk with a pencil.

"Neither Lawrence nor Halsey had money to finance a salvage operation, so Lawrence contacted Sheldon Posner. And my guess is Lawrence couldn't resist telling Donna Ingram, who told her father, Mo Carver."

"Why did Williams buy a hacksaw?"

"The guy had cancer and no insurance. He wanted to provide for his wife. He knew the location where he salvaged the Queen's Jewels with Halsey. After Halsey's murder, Ossie realized he couldn't raise the gold statue alone. What he could do is hack it up into salvageable pieces."

Fernandez's cell phone rang.

"Frank," Vesta said.

"Hold it, I'm putting you on the speakerphone."

"You were right. Mo Carver served time in the Florida State Prison in Radford. Carver claimed one of the guards broke the knuckles on his right hand with a T-baton nightstick like the Los Angeles Police used on Rodney King. The guard's name was Raymond Santiago. He was fired for physically abusing inmates."

"Thanks."

Fernandez hung up and continued. "Carver was first mate on the *Calusa*. He spotted Santiago and Posner coming on board. He recognized Santiago as the Radford guard who had smashed his fingers and ruined his career.

"Mo Carver was an underwater demolition expert in Nam. He set two small explosive charges, enough to disable the ship, but close enough to shore to preclude anyone being killed.

"What Carver didn't know was there would be a sudden gale. He helped Collins steer the boat. Then he killed Santiago for revenge. If the ship were scuttled, Santiago's body would be at the bottom of the sea."

VESTA RANG AGAIN.

"Frank, Fed Ex dropped off a package addressed to you. It's from a funeral home in Carmel, California."

"It's Ellie St. Clair's ashes."

TEN MINUTES LATER FRANK OPENED the package and scanned the enclosed letter from a California law firm.

Dear Mr. Fernandez:

I regret to inform you that Ellen St. Clair died at 11 p.m. August 5 at the Community Hospital of the Monterrey Peninsula. Mrs. St. Clair provided our law firm with explicit instructions for her cremation and burial. She requested her ashes were to be scattered in the ocean near Fort Pierce where she grew up.

Police Chief Louis Brumberg volunteered the good offices of his department. He recommended that you be entrusted with carrying out arrangements for Ellen St. Clair's final request.

Please forward receipts for accrued expenses to my attention.

Very truly yours,
Richard Carlson

...42

FRANK FERNANDEZ'S HEART ACHED over the death of Ellie St. Clair, over the loss of something that might have been. He let out a deep sigh of melancholy and choked back emotions as he waded into the surf. He raised the solid rosewood box to his lips, kissed it, and upended the container of ashes. A west wind kicked up. Ellie's ashes wafted over the water, drifting off from Frederick Douglass Beach.

Fernandez hadn't noticed the approach of the boat that drifted silently on shore without lights. He recognized the glint of metal in the moonlight. He heard an explosion like the crack of a whip and felt a rush of fire in his left shoulder. The agony was enormous.

Tears filled his eyes, stinging. Fernandez blinked them away and staggered back to the beach, dropping down against a sand dune. He remained silent, trying to staunch the flow of blood from the wound with his handkerchief.

Minutes passed. He heard whispered voices and saw a shadow fall across him in the first rays of dawn. Fernandez sensed movement, but he didn't hear or see anything before a heavy pistol butt hit him.

I can't die like this, he thought, trying to raise a defensive arm above his head. But he was unable to move a single limb—his left side was paralyzed. The man was over 6 feet tall. There was no judgment on his face. He might have been waiting for a bus.

Fernandez tried to speak through dry, sandy lips. "Collins—"

The second blow to the face broke his nose. The darkness crept in from the outer edges of his field of vision. He was passing out in a slow, dreamy way, sliding down and down into darkness.

A chilling bird hiss filled the silence.

A shiver ran over Fernandez's scalp as he saw Skip Collins' finger tighten on the trigger. He hunched his shoulders and squeezed his eyes closed. Reflexively, he lowered his head, his thoughts a swirling tempest of fear and regret.

CRACK. CRACK. Fernandez's nerve synapses fired into his brain—unable to compute. Opening his eyes, he saw Mo Carver, a glazed look in his eyes, blood seeping from a bullet hole in the center of his forehead. Carver's body slid to the sand, blood pooling on the beach.

"Improvise," Skip Collins chuckled. "Improvise. I just dissolved a partnership. You will be a hero, Fernandez. Your name will go on an FBI wall somewhere. You died in a shootout with a serial killer. I will be off the coast of Ireland, salvaging the *Lusitania*. For now, let me put this gun in your hand; then I'll put you out of your misery."

He felt his strength ebbing.

Collins grinned as he placed the empty gun in Fernandez's hand.

In the fading twilight of his consciousness, Frank imagined he heard the flapping wings of a huge bird.

In desperation, Fernandez's legs lashed out, catching the big man off balance. Collins fell on top of him, cursing.

Fernandez fumbled in his pocket for his penknife. Somehow he managed to keep a grip on the slippery handle. His fingers were stiffening, as though the blood supply was cutting off. Ignoring the pain, Fernandez held his knife, using both hands in an ice pick grip. He stabbed Collins in the neck, pumping his hands up and down, again and again, until he could no longer lift the knife. His reflexes failed him.

Collins' expression went blank. The fatal knife thrusts into the base of his skull had severed his spinal cord. Collins was dead.

Fernandez opened his eyes. He looked down and saw the deep red stains spread on his shirtfront. Somehow he had survived.

AT SUNRISE ON SUNDAY, Greg Picard drove the four-wheeler on his daily patrol, searching for nesting sea turtles on the beach. Approaching Frederick Douglass Beach, he rubbed his eyes. Two dead men were sprawled on the beach, and another man was covered in blood, but still breathing.

"My shoulder," Fernandez mumbled and coughed.

"I'll get you an ambulance," Picard said.

"I won't make it—"

"Yes, you will. Lie still. The ambulance will be here soon." Greg Picard wiped blood from Fernandez's mouth with his shirtsleeve.

Fernandez felt it coming: the chill and dizziness. It started in his feet and hands. It spread to his head. And darkness followed.

Two Dead, One Injured in Shootout

FORT PIERCE—A Sunday morning struggle on Hutchinson Island ended with a serial killer suspect and his accomplice being killed, and a Fort Pierce police consultant suffering non-life-threatening injuries.

Around 7:15 a.m. Greg Picard, a member of the volunteer Fort Pierce Turtle Patrol, was driving his beach vehicle on South Hutchinson Island. As Picard approached Frederick Douglass Park, he heard moaning, saw three men covered in blood, and called 911. Picard then offered first aid to the wounded survivor, Frank Fernandez.

The two dead men were identified as Moses Carver and Skipper Collins. Collins was a prime suspect in the unsolved Fort Pierce serial murders of Campbell Lawrence, Halsey White and Ossie Williams.

According to police, when the incident occurred, Collins and Carver were illegally salvaging in the area of the 1715 Spanish treasure shipwreck off Frederick Douglass Park.

Detective Frank Fernandez surprised the two poachers, resulting in Collins firing a high-caliber handgun and wounding Fernandez in the shoulder. Apparently, Carver and Collins had a falling-out and Collins shot his co-conspirator in the head, killing him instantly.

Police Chief Louis Brumberg said that Collins had attempted to place the handgun in Fernandez's hand when the unarmed and seriously wounded ex-FBI man, using only a penknife, was able to strike a deadly blow to Collins' carotid artery.

Fort Pierce Mayor Willie Westlake said, "This situation proves that by outsourcing law enforcement services, the city will save money and deliver results."

...44

"HOW ARE YOU FEELING THIS MORNING? My name is Dr. Rai." The tall, dark-completed doctor of Indian ancestry glanced at Frank Fernandez's chart.

"My, my, what a difficulty you have experienced."

"How soon can I leave?"

His warm smile evaporated. "I don't expect you to be walking around good as new for a while. The x-ray films showed the bullet removed from your shoulder had breached the network of nerves that sent signals from your spine to your shoulder and caused your temporary paralysis.

"Gunshot victims with brachial plexus wounds usually require follow-up surgery to deal with blood vessel damage, pain, and loss of motor function. Be patient, Mr. Fernandez. Let's see how you do in you physical therapy."

Dr. Rai used his iPhone flashlight to study Fernandez's face. "Your nose is swollen. Does it affect your breathing?"

"No."

"Good. I reset the bone while you were in surgery. At home, use a bag of ice or frozen peas across your nose as well as head elevation to reduce swelling.

"If you experience bleeding, apply pressure with your thumb and forefinger for 15 minutes without letting go."

"What do I take for pain?"

"Tylenol is best."

"How about hydrocodone?"

"Effective but addictive."

Fernandez watched the doctor's eyes. He had spent his career watching eyes. Dr. Rai was holding back something.

"What haven't you told me?"

The doctor paused. "You have a preexisting condition. Correct?"

Fernandez was silent.

"The films also showed an interarticular invasion of two bullet fragments, and your blood tests established that you have microcytic anemia with very high blood lead levels."

"Give it to me in plain English."

"Exposed adults should have blood lead levels below 40 micrograms. Yours is greater than 90. I recommend that you start on chelation therapy immediately."

Fernandez swallowed, but he had no saliva.

"My brother is a doctor at Hopkins. He told me there is a risk of heart problems associated with chelation therapy. In addition, there is a chance that therapy could result in kidney failure—which would require dialysis."

"All of that is true; nevertheless—"

Fernandez broke in. "Thank you, Dr. Rai."

After the doctor left, Fernandez started to get out of bed. He experienced a stab of pain in his shoulder; a shiver and a chill passed through him. He bit his lip in silence.

"HOW'S THE HERO of Frederick Douglass Park?" Miriam Jolson said. "How's your shoulder?"

"The doctors are talking surgery. Depends on how I do in physical therapy."

She placed the tips of her fingers together. "May I ask you questions—off the record?"

"Of course."

"Why were you at Frederick Douglass Beach?"

"It was Sunday. I wanted to deposit Ellie St. Clair's ashes in private, before the beachgoers showed up."

"Why Frederick Douglass?"

The medical examiner asked questions in a calm yet firm voice, like someone who was used to getting answers. Fernandez shrugged but didn't respond. The movement caused a spasm of pain in his shoulder.

Jolson narrowed her eyes. "From what I understand, Collins and his first mate Carver appeared. Right?"

"Right."

"Collins then shot you in the right shoulder."

"Go on."

"Why shoot you for dumping ashes in the water?"

Without waiting for a reply, she added, "Your doctor said the shot paralyzed your shoulder."

He nodded.

"And then for some unexplained reason, Collins shot his companion in the head. Still with me?"

"OK."

"Where did you get the penknife?"

"Walmart."

"You told Chief Brumberg you temporarily passed out from loss of blood and you were delusionary, but when Collins tried to plant the handgun on you, you managed to cause him to stumble. The linebacker-size guy fell on top of you, and somehow you were able to open your little Chinese-made Walmart penknife and cut his carotid artery. Still with me, Frank?"

He didn't respond.

"I'm a forensic scientist. I find it passing strange that someone shot in the brachial plexus that controlled his arm function could, while semi-conscious, open a penknife and stick it through the carotid artery of a man weighing over 200 pounds and then jerk it around some until the man bled to death.

"Contrary to popular belief, human beings are very hard to instantly kill. Yet somehow you managed. I'm impressed."

"Where are you going with all this, Miriam?"

"I did the autopsy on Collins. The man's carotid artery was slashed by what looked to me like a powerful claw or a sharp, hooked beak, not a two-dollar penknife."

Jolson leaned over and whispered, "If I reported Collins was killed by a vulture, they would fire me. I know that somebody or something was on the beach with you."

He remained mute.

She kissed him on the forehead. "I love you, Fernandez. If I preferred men, you would be at the top of my list. You're a good guy, but a lousy liar."

THE FOLLOWING AFTERNOON a nurse brought a wheelchair. She guided her patient to the hospital entrance. Lou Brumberg waited in a police car. Frank Fernandez struggled to buckle the seat belt over his shoulder bandage. It was painful.

"Thanks for picking me up, Lou."

"You up for stopping at Archie's for a hamburger?"

"No appetite. Thanks."

The police chief looked him in the eye. It was the kind of look that meant Brumberg was serious.

"What's bothering you, Lou?"

"I'm worried."

Fernandez waited for him to continue.

"I heard from Manion. The FBI is looking for Ray Santiago in connection with Abu Ghraib. An Al Jazeera journalist who was a former prisoner filed a lawsuit against Flintlock USA, the private contractor that ran the prison. Santiago was named ringleader of the Flintlock employees working at Abu Ghraib. Santiago allegedly subjected the plaintiff to severe physical abuse. He's been subpoenaed. The FBI is seeking information regarding his whereabouts."

"Why are you worried?"

With an edge to his voice, Brumberg said, "You and I have a good idea where Santiago's body is. I'm an officer of the court. Mo Carver had a revenge motive to kill Santiago. I'm obligated to pass that information along. I like my job as chief of police, and I can't afford a serious miscalculation."

"Is the insurance company going to raise the *Calusa*?"

"Doubtful. Derechos are natural disasters, or 'acts of God,' and are not covered."

"Let me help you with your irresolvable moral dilemma. Do you have a witness who can testify Santiago is at the bottom of the Fort Pierce Inlet?"

Brumberg did not reply.

"Do you have forensic evidence?"

"Your point?"

"That storm was powerful enough to bury Santiago's body deep in the sand. Stop worrying."

The police chief drove in silence.

"I handled this case like an amateur," Fernandez said. "I thought we were looking for a serial murderer. When I questioned Posner and Santiago, I was focused on Campbell Lawrence's murder. Both had solid alibis. I didn't question them about Halsey White's death. I was off in different directions.

"Vesta contacted the St. Lucie County Airport. Talon Air is a jet charter service. They handled a flight from New York to Fort Pierce in the early a.m. on the day Halsey was killed. Without a subpoena, Talon Air wouldn't release the passenger's identity.

"I know it was Santiago. The man was psychotic. He proved it in Abu Ghraib and again in Radford Prison. In the FBI we studied serial killers, the psychotic and the psychopathic. The psychotic is legally insane; they can't tell the difference between right and wrong. The psychopath knows the difference between right and wrong—just doesn't care. They have no conscience, or their conscience is too weak to stop violent behavior. A guy like Santiago would have felt no guilt or remorse."

Neither man spoke until they passed the guard gate at Ocean Village. As he pulled up to Fernandez's condominium entrance, Brumberg said, "No witnesses, no proof or forensics. Nothing except more educated guessing."

"I'm not one of your detectives any longer, Lou, but I'll throw one more educated guess in—for free. Moses Carver killed Campbell Lawrence and then scuttled his boat to eliminate evidence of his daughter ever being on board. He did it out of love."

"Good motive."

"Think for a second. If someone raped your daughter, you would want to strangle the bastard. Right?"

The chief didn't respond.

"The mother of your hatred would be love. It's love that makes people do things to prevent harm to their family. Lawrence seduced Donna Ingram, although I don't think it took much doing. When Donna told her father, Mo Carver, she was pregnant, he freaked out.

"Carver loved his daughter. He couldn't see her throwing her life away on a drifter like Lawrence. He did what he thought he had to do."

"Thank you, Dr. Freud, for sharing that shaft of brilliant insight." Brumberg coughed. "I have been requested by our esteemed mayor to renew your consulting contract."

"Lou, you know he only wants to piggyback on the newspaper publicity to prove his outsourcing program works. That's bullshit. After twenty years working for the FBI, I don't plan to swap one bureaucracy for another."

"You disappoint me. Where's your integrity?"

"Whatever I had left is used up, Lou. All used up." Fernandez sighed wearily. "And I'm used up too."

...46

IN THE OCEAN HOUSE LOBBY, Frank Fernandez picked up his newspaper and took the elevator to his second floor apartment. He fixed a cup of coffee and settled on the deck. An article in the business section of the *Times* captured his attention.

Management Changes at Lazarus Corporation

STAMFORD— Following the tragic death of CEO Sheldon Posner in a boating mishap in Florida, the directors of the Lazarus Corporation chose Meryl Rothstein to lead the company. "Our objective is to improve relations with citizens in the Black Lake region," Rothstein said.

Recently, Peruvian citizens filled the town square in Cajamarca, the city closest to the mine, protesting the mine's plans to expand operations into a mountain called Cerro Quilish. For campesinos, Cerro Quilish is a sacred mountain and a source of precious water. Local residents also opposed expansion of the mine after a toxic mercury spill by Lazarus led to health problems in their community.

Rothstein flew to Peru to meet with Catholic priest and local activist Father Dominic Affuso. She agreed to suspend mining operations into Cerro Quilish. Rothstein said that she hoped the mine will be a neighbor here for a very long time, and on behalf of Lazarus, Rothstein pledged

Yanacocha, the world's richest gold mine, will henceforth operate using U.S. environmental and ethical standards.

Wall Street reacted favorably to the news.

...47

AT 6:45 A.M. FRANK FERNANDEZ SAT bolt upright in bed. It took a few seconds before he realized it was his own scream of pain that had woken him. Then he laid his head back on the pillow, massaging his shoulder and throbbing nose.

He turned on the light, filled a paper cup with water, and downed two hydrocodone tablets. In the kitchen he searched for milk for his coffee. He didn't take it black anymore, probably a sign of getting old.

Settling in a comfortable chair in his living room, Fernandez drank his coffee in slow sips. He thought of Robert Manion. As Vesta had suggested, he had done the numbers, and the young FBI agent could very well be his son—his ghost son. It would profit no one to pursue the subject. The result would be bitterness, recrimination, and embarrassment for Clara Manion.

Fernandez's mind wandered to his own ghost son, Charles, living in Sarasota with Maris. Sarasota. Where he could have been. Where maybe he should have been. Where now that Maris was in a new relationship, he would never be. What had Ellie advised? "Pull up your socks, get over it; make an effort with the kid." The pills made him drowsy. He really had to cut back on the narcotics.

Frank closed his eyes. He caught a scent of perfume. *White Jasmine.* A vibration went through him. When he opened his eyes, Isabel was seated next to him, smiling. Fernandez felt his chest constrict. An erection began to throb against his shorts. Isabel raised an eyebrow as if she sensed it too. Her eyes were dark, piercing, unreadable. Her hair was so intensely black that it was almost blue.

Isabel was dressed as an Inca princess, wearing a series of cords wound around her neck with a fringe of scarlet tassels at her ankles and a headdress of long, shiny black feathers.

His pulse was racing. "Isabel, I saw you on the beach praying for lightning and thunder. Did you destroy the *Calusa*?"

There was a sardonic smile on her lips. It was in her eyes—a quick something that flashed. He had stepped over some imaginary line.

"Where Inca blood is shed, the tree of forgiveness doesn't grow. The greedy Spanish devils hid behind their crosses. They forced Atahualpa to convert to their church and then betrayed him. Pizarro ordered Atahualpa strangled and a pyre made of his sacred corpse to prevent our king from traveling to the afterlife. When Atahualpa's body turned to ashes, the Inca nation lost its greatness."

He was hypnotized by her words.

"Then the Spanish king ordered an idol forged from Incan gold to pay honor to the church that murdered Atahualpa."

Fernandez broke in. "The Golden Madonna was lost for 300 years. What difference would it have made if the statue ended up in some church in Spain?"

A strange grunt escaped Isabel's mouth. "To forget one's ancestors is to be a brook without a source, a tree without a root."

"Isabel, was it you who killed Collins on the beach?"

She narrowed her dark, piercing eyes, but remained silent. In the pale yellow lamplight, her copper skin and black hair framed her exotically beautiful face.

Isabel rose. She kissed him gently on the lips. "The condor teaches if you wish to climb high, you have to do it against the wind."

And then *Isabel Sancho de Rojas Atahualpa* was gone.

FRANK FERNANDEZ SHOOK HIS HEAD to rid his imagination of the vengeful Inca princess or animal-human hybrid or whatever she was. In the ensuing silence he heard a high-pitched screech.

It was daybreak.

He walked out onto his deck overlooking the sea. The ocean looked a deep metallic blue until it broke in foamy-white pulses on the shore. An offshore breeze picked up. As Frank stood watching, the morning sky changed from blood red to violet to bright orange and finally to a brilliant golden-yellow. He shielded his eyes from the sun.

A spine-chilling hiss punctured the silence. He stared unbelieving at the sight of a large condor perched on the sand dune. He felt like pinching himself to make sure he wasn't dreaming.

With a sharp cry, the bird took off, slicing through the air, dipping her ten-foot wingspan in Frank's direction in a solitary salute before soaring high over the Atlantic, becoming a small black silhouette in the sky.

He returned to his living room. On the chair where Isabel had been sitting, he spotted something. Carefully he picked it up. It was a long black feather. Frank raised it to his nose. *White Jasmine.*

Epilogue

ON AUGUST 7, A STORM that meteorologists called a *derecho* hit the Florida coast at Hutchinson Island near Fort Pierce. Derechos are warm-weather phenomena occurring mostly in summer, especially during July and August. The U.S. National Oceanic and Atmospheric Administration (NOAA) reported the rare August mega-thunderstorm lasted 30 minutes, producing damaging winds as high as 168 mph, causing tornado-like damage and erosion on nearby beaches.

A reef line runs parallel to shore east of Hutchinson Island. During the recent derecho, energetic waves scoured the beach, transporting metric tons of sand to the offshore rocky ridge just off Frederick Douglass Beach.

The sandy avalanche caused by the derecho covered one huge section of waterlogged timber that had shifted during Hurricane Jeanne. As a result, the faint glimmer of an eight-foot statue of solid gold was no longer visible on the ocean floor.

Acknowledgements

I wish to express appreciation to Robby McCurry for introducing me to the story of the 1715 Spanish Plate Fleet. As a former part-time treasure salvor, Robby provided invaluable information about shipwreck exploration.

To the Collection of Gisela Fabian for permitting use of *Revenge* by Riguad Benoit, one of the most influential names in Haitian Art.

To the David Rumsey Map Collection for permitting the use of *The Map of the West Indies, Mexico and New Spain.*

Thanks to Scott Mahr, who was responsible for creating the book jacket, maps and all interior graphics.

And to my editor, Jennifer Adkins, for her gifted talent and kindness.

Last on the list to acknowledge are the intrepid treasure hunters who are still out there seeking the Golden Madonna and the tons of gold, silver and other valuable historical artifacts buried on the bottom of the sea.

As Captain Halsey White said, "Let me tell you something. Treasure hunting is one of the most exciting adventures left on earth."

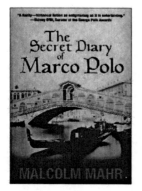
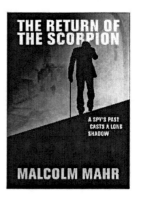

THE GOLDEN MADONNA

FRANK FERNANDEZ MYSTERY SERIES

The Orange Blossom Mob

Five geriatric mobsters retire to Florida and volunteer their special talents to aid police in lowering the crime rate.

The Einstein Project

In Jerusalem, an American is murdered. Two days earlier, in the Arabian Sea an eerie bolt of lightning struck an Israeli warship. An Islamic terrorist group claimed responsibility. Former FBI agent Frank Fernandez delves deeper into the two mysteries leading to a shocking scientific discovery and a conspiracy of staggering brilliance.

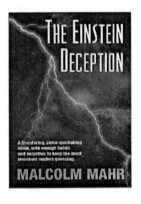

The Hostage

The President asks retired FBI agent Frank Fernandez to investigate the disappearance of her elderly mother from a Fort Pierce nursing facility. Fernandez can trust no one as he tries to discover who is behind the plot to destabilize the American Presidency.

CPSIA information can be obtained at www.ICGtesting.com
Printed in the USA
LVOW10s1150070416

482569LV00001B/4/P